LORD OF THE FRIES

LORD OF THE FRIES

L. S. KINNEDY

RAZORBILL

RAZORBILL

An imprint of Penguin Random House LLC
New York

First published in the United States of America by Razorbill,
an imprint of Penguin Random House LLC, 2019

Visit us online at penguinrandomhouse.com

LIBRARY OF CONGRESS CATALOGING-IN-PUBLICATION DATA IS AVAILABLE

ISBN 9780593202616

Printed in the United States of America

1 3 5 7 9 10 8 6 4 2

Design by Maria Santa.
Text set in Diverda Serif Com.

To Laura, a wizard of words,

a master of story,

the most impressive spinner of

potato-based tales.

CHAPTER 1

CRASH, FLASH, BOOM!

My friends and I are like soldiers having a last night on the town before heading out to war. Only, the "town" is a potato field in Upstate New York. And the "war" is middle school.

"I wish we could have a bonfire," I groan to my best friends, Kayla Jeffers and Felipe Ramos. "What good is a campout without s'mores toasted over an open fire?"

"I don't know, Spud, raw s'mores aren't half bad," Kayla says as she munches on graham crackers, cold chocolate, and unmelted marshmallows.

"Besides," Felipe adds, "if we had a fire it would kill our night vision. Just look at all those stars!"

He flops onto his back so he can admire the view. "I should have brought my telescope."

The real reason we can't have a fire is because Mom and Dad don't trust me.

"It's not that we don't trust you," Mom told me when I whined for a campfire for the millionth time. "We don't trust luck. What if the wind picks up and a spark gets into the field? The entire crop could be destroyed. Or what if you fall asleep and the fire gets to the barn and burns up Tooba?" She shuddered at the thought.

See, they don't trust me. Do they really think I'm going to do anything that would put Tooba at risk? I mean, Tooba is the most important thing to my family. And as for the potato crop, well, potatoes are my whole life.

Unfortunately.

My parents gave up sixty-hour work weeks in the city to buy this plot of land in Upstate New York, just outside the state forest, and close to the little town of Solanum. They had a dream of a simple, natural life.

When they were thinking about what to plant, Mom asked me, "What's your favorite vegetable?"

I didn't even have to think about it. "French fries!"

I was six, okay? I didn't know.

But after Mom and Dad stopped laughing, they realized it was a brilliant idea. Americans might talk about kale smoothies, but what they really eat, what they really love, are fries.

Kale stars in the Instagram photos when people want to say *Look how healthy I am*.

Potatoes are what they swallow by the ton.

So we started a potato farm. It went pretty well, but New York isn't exactly known for its tubers. Idaho is the real potato powerhouse. It wasn't easy, and we'll never be rich, but we sold our spuds at farmers markets and a couple of local stores, and we made it work.

Then Mom found Tooba.

The mother potato.

After that, our life was all potatoes all the time.

And our potatoes are perfect.

They're big, with thin skins. Their insides are this wonderful buttery golden color. And once you dunk them in sizzling oil they turn into the crunchiest, tastiest fries the world has ever known. Puffy on the inside, crispy on the outside, they take fast food to a cosmic level.

And even though our food truck—Lord of the Fries, Dad's idea—offers ketchup, mustard, and that weird cheese curd mix Canadians like, no one ever dips our fries in anything. Even Felipe, who can't have a normal fry without dunking it in pickle juice, eats our fries plain. They don't even need salt!

My real name is Sampson, but as soon as he met me, Felipe nicknamed me Spud, and it stuck. So now, not only is my entire home life dominated by potatoes—my identity is a potato, too!

When we've eaten all the raw s'mores we can eat, I yawn and say, "Well, guess it's time to sleep." I'm already crawling into the big tent when Kayla and Felipe start to laugh at me.

"Early birds!" Kayla squeals.

"Early birds!" Felipe shouts back, and they start making these ridiculous tweeting sounds.

"What are you guys talking about?" I ask.

"Oh, just something from kindergarten. Remember Miss McGriff? How she used to . . ." Kayla dissolves in giggles.

I just stare at them. I know if I ask what *early birds* is about they'll just have some lame story that doesn't seem funny to me. I didn't meet either of them until second grade, but they've known each other forever. As in, waddled around in diapers back in the day. Traded pacifiers. There's even a photo of them in the bathtub together, age two, that Kayla's mom brings out at every one of Kayla's birthday parties.

Kayla and Felipe also live in town, right next door to each other, and can hang out whenever they want. I live in the back end of nowhere, a half-hour bike ride away. I have to practically get a signed permission slip to visit them.

Felipe and Kayla are my best friends, but sometimes it feels like I'm out of their friendship orbit because I live so far away. That, and I'm always helping out mom and dad with the potatoes. It's 24/7 taters down at the farm.

"You can't be tired," Felipe complains. "It's only ten o'clock. If we were at my house, Kayla and I would be up another two hours watching the *Mutant Fruit from Planet Poot* marathon on the Syfy channel."

"Well, I *am* tired," I snap back. "Unlike you and Kayla, who spent the whole summer watching movies and fiddling with electronics, I had to work. Summer might be relaxing for you, but for us it's tourist season. That means I get up early and peel potatoes. Like a billion potatoes! And then cut potatoes, 'cause the sign on our truck says 'hand cut.' Guess whose hands?" I wiggle my fingers in their faces.

My voice is getting louder and louder. My friends are looking at me like I'm crazy, but I can't stop. "And then I fry the stinking potatoes!" I jump up, shaking my fists at the fields. "And I do mean stinking. Do you realize I've spent the last four years smelling like a French fry?"

I've worn myself out with my sudden frustration. Exhausted, I flop down by my friends.

No one says anything for a while.

Then finally Kayla smiles and punches me on the shoulder. "So I guess you're the only one of us who's actually excited for middle school to start."

"Yeah," Felipe says. "School will be your vacation from work."

I laugh, because it's both true and sad. "Sure, I just can't wait for classes to start," I say sarcastically. "So much to look forward to. I'll trade in peelers for lockers that won't open. Swap out oil stains for giant eighth graders with facial hair."

"Seven classes, seven teachers, seven homework assignments!" Felipe moans.

"Bullies and peer pressure and . . ." Kayla's voice drops to a whisper. "Hormones!"

"Oh gosh, it's going to be terrible, isn't it?" I say. "And it's only three days away."

"Two," Kayla corrects. "Today's over, so there's just Saturday and Sunday, and then . . ."

"Off to war!" I salute.

"Don't worry, guys," Felipe says. "We'll be okay. I mean, we've got each other. So even if everyone else is a bully or a jerk, we'll do just fine."

"Yeah," Kayla says. "As long as we have each other, nothing can go wrong."

We stay up for a while talking about middle school, sounding much braver than we feel. Around midnight we finally crawl into the spacious tent my dad helped me set up. I fall asleep almost at once, bone-tired.

It feels like only minutes later I'm jolted awake by a flash that looks like lightning, followed by a huge BOOM louder than any thunder. I bolt upright, looking around in the dark. "What the . . ."

"Is it raining?" Kayla asks groggily from her sleeping bag.

"I don't think so," I say, reaching for the tent zipper. "The forecast said clear skies, and believe me, a farmer pays attention to the weather."

Felipe is snoring, somehow still sleeping. I poke him in the ribs with my big toe. "Felipe, wake up. Something happened."

I crawl out of the tent and look around. I have to admit, the potato fields look beautiful in the moonlight. The purple flowers tucked amid the dark green leaves seem to shimmer under the twinkling stars. And I know that under each mound of dirt are the golden tubers that will help our family thrive for another year.

"Was it a car crash?" Kayla asks, crawling out behind me.

"No, the main road's really far away," I say. "This sounded close. In the fields, maybe."

My heart races as I think of losing the crops. The fence keeps out rabbits and whistle-pigs, but if someone wanted to sabotage the crop . . .

Someone like a jerky neighbor who also started growing potatoes soon after Lord of the Fries became successful . . .

"We have to check on Tooba, then check the

fields," I say. "Felipe, are you awake yet? Get the Adventure Bag!"

Felipe, Kayla, and I first packed the Adventure Bag when we were seven. We filled it with everything we could possibly need—water, beef jerky, hammer, flashlight, shovel, notebook, compass, bandages, towel—and took it absolutely everywhere. I mean, even if we went to the Super Mart for an Icicle Slush we had this thirty-pound bag with us.

We thought it was the coolest thing ever.

Now, I don't know. I'm almost embarrassed we still have it. It seems like such a little-kid thing. Middle schoolers don't have adventures. They have homework and stress.

I see the light flash on Felipe's watch. "It's two a.m.! This isn't a good time for an adventure," he says.

"No, it's a *great* time for an adventure!" I say, suddenly wide awake. "Come on!"

Whatever this might be, at least it's better than worrying about middle school, or whether our friendship will last. Or smelling like a freshly fried French fry.

I put a finger to my lips. "Shh, we don't want to wake my parents," I caution as we sneak out of the tent. I pitched it as far from the house as my parents would allow, but it is still close enough that loud voices could potentially wake them. There are coyotes and black bears and bobcats out here, and they didn't want us too far away in case something happened. But I think they wanted us close because, like I said before, they don't really trust me.

We're close to the barn where Tooba lives. Parked next to the barn is Lord of the Fries, the camper that Dad converted to a food truck. Let's just say that our food truck looks a lot better in the dark. By daylight it doesn't look very professional. There are rust holes, a big dent in one side, and one taillight that never works. "But it is completely sanitary!" Mom always assures nervous customers. "That's not dirt, just stains."

Beyond the barn and food truck is an open stretch of fallow land, and then the fenced fields.

Felipe tosses me the Adventure Bag, and we head toward the barn. We don't get very far before I notice something strange ahead of us.

"Look, is that someone with a flashlight?" I point at the light coming from the farthest side of the field.

"Maybe," Kayla says, peering into the darkness.

"No, it's not moving," I say. "And it's an odd color." The light is pulsing a strange green-blue.

I gulp, frightened and excited, and whisper, *"There's something weird in the potato field!"*

CHAPTER 2

MY GREAT-AUNT TOOBA

Remember when you were a little kid, and as soon as anything happened you ran to your parents? Like, *anything.* If you bit your tongue. If there was a clown on TV. If the old man next door called you "my fine feathered friend" and you didn't know what it meant but you worried you might be secretly growing feathers.

You ran to them because you wanted them to save you, to fix everything. But eventually you learned that except for really big things—actual broken bones, small explosions—there wasn't really all that much they could do.

Parents are really good at saying, "Oh, sweetie, you'll be okay! I love you!" and giving hugs and kisses. Sometimes lollipops. And that's great. For most things that happen to you when you're five years old, that works.

But when you get older, you figure out that these methods don't solve all of your problems. So by the time you're eleven, like me, you've learned not to run to your parents the second something upsetting happens. At best, you get the hugs and then your problems are still there.

At worst, you wind up getting grounded.

So when my friends and I see that weird glowing thing in the potato field, it never occurs to me to run and wake up my parents. In fact, the main thing on my mind is to *not* wake them up. Whenever anything goes wrong, their first thought is to blame me. We run out of fries while the line gets longer? You should have peeled faster, Spud. The Lord of the Fries food truck doesn't start? Did you leave the headlights on and drain the battery again, Spud? Spud, why have the lines at Lord of the Fries gotten shorter and shorter? Why isn't the credit card reader working? Spud? Spud? *Spud!*

Okay, some of those things are *technically* my fault but not all! And isn't a kid allowed a few mess-ups?

"Let's go see what it is," Felipe says excitedly.

"Hold on," I say. "We have to check on Tooba first."

Sometimes when I'm talking about Tooba I feel like I'm talking about an old family member, like a long-lost great auntie whom we reconnected with. We worry a lot about her comfort and happiness, if the air is too hot or too cold, if she wants some bedtime tea.

The barn door has a lock on it, but I know the combination. "See," Kayla points out as I spin the lock. "All ready for middle school."

"I don't know why you're so worried about opening a locker," I say as I flub the combination and have to start all over. "I mean, you can fix computers. You can *make* computers. How hard can a simple lock be for you?"

"BECAUSE WE ONLY HAVE THREE MINUTES BETWEEN CLASSES!" she explodes. Then she takes a deep breath and apologizes. "Science is slow. Engineering is careful. But when I have to do something fast my hands start to shake and I just can't do it!"

"My mom told me a trick," Felipe says. "Each time you close your lock, you do the first two numbers of the combination again. Then you set up the spinny thing just a few clicks away from the third number."

Kayla's eyes light up. "That way, if I'm in a hurry next time, I just have to turn the lock a little bit and . . . viola!"

"Violin!" Felipe shouts.

"Cello!" Kayla counters.

"Bass fiddle!"

"It's not 'viola,'" I tell her, frustrated because all their chattering is making me forget the combination now. "It's *voilà*. It's French, I think."

"Oh I know, silly," Kayla scoffs. "It's just we watched this space musical this week at Felipe's and—"

"And the main robot was trying to learn the difference between all the stringed instruments. She recited the list, and viola, which is a little bigger than a violin, was last on the list."

"So she ended with *violin, viola, voilà!*" Felipe finishes, and the two of them dissolve into giggles.

I don't get the joke. "It's not really all that funny," I point out.

My comment makes them stop laughing. "I know," Kayla says, and shrugs. "It was funny when we watched it, though. You know how it is."

No, I don't, I want to say. I feel like such an outsider right now because I don't get it. It's like someone has hung a neon sign around my neck that blinks LEFT OUT. LEFT OUT. LEFT OUT. I'm the farmer boy who lives at the back end of nowhere and has to work instead of being a regular kid.

I shouldn't feel bad about their close friendship. They never deliberately exclude me and I do really think we're all best friends. No *best* and *bester* and *bestest*. I guess it's just that people always talk about having one singular best friend. So sometimes I feel like Felipe and Kayla are best friends, and I'm just a very good friend to both of them.

And it's not like I don't have special moments with each of them individually. Felipe became my friend first, and we have plenty of adventures together while Kayla is home breaking gizmos and appliances so she can put them together again. We ride all around the county with our Adventure Bag, jumping ditches, catching snakes, with Felipe getting us into trouble and me getting us out again.

And I have a close bond with Kayla, too. Sometimes when Felipe is at the university where his parents work, I hang out with Kayla at her noisy, crowded, unruly house. She complains about it all the time, but I think how amazing it would be to have four brothers and sisters—built-in friends. "Built-in enemies is more like it," Kayla grumbles, but I know her family is loving and supportive, even if it's also chaotic.

So why do I feel like the third wheel right now?

Finally, I get the lock open, and we slip into the barn.

There Tooba rests, in all her potato-y splendor. Basking in the palest silver glow, she sleeps in her specially designed hydroponic chamber, growing and dreaming of little baby tubers.

"Wow, she's gotten even bigger since the last time I saw her," Felipe comments.

"You saw her right after planting," I tell him. "Now she's had a few months to heal."

Tooba is the size of a basketball now. By the time we're ready to harvest pieces from her again, she'll be the size of a beach ball.

"I still don't understand how that works," Felipe says, scratching his head as he admires plump Tooba. "Those potato plants out there have flowers, right? So that must mean they make seeds too."

Luckily he's asked the potato expert. "They do

technically produce seeds, sometimes. But not all the time. If the weather is too hot, or too cold, or too dry, or too wet . . . er, too just about anything, the flowers just die without making seeds. But the real problem is that seeds aren't predictable."

"Well, what in life is?" Kayla asks, sounding like a philosopher.

"Actual potatoes are," I tell her. "With seeds, you never know what the plant will come out like, whether the potatoes will be any good. Each one is different. But if you plant a piece of the original potato, the baby will be an exact clone of the mother potato."

"Like in *Clone Clowns of the Cosmos*!" Felipe says. "The worst horror/sci-fi movie known to man."

"And you've watched it how many times?" I tease him.

"Well, three. Or eight. But c'mon, it had some interesting ideas. Like the way you can't clone a clone."

"You can clone a clown, but can't clone a clown clone?" I ask. "Yeah, that information will be really helpful in your future life."

"So you don't want variety in your potatoes, is that what you're saying?" Kayla asks.

"Right," I tell her. "We want every potato to be exactly like Tooba. So for each new plant we need, we have to cut a tiny slice from Tooba."

Felipe shudders. "It sounds weird to talk about cutting parts of her off. It's like she's a member of your family, the way you talk about her."

"Well, I don't think it hurts her," I say. "She's never complained about it!"

"And you can cut off as many pieces as you need?" Kayla asks.

"Not really. With most potatoes, you need to have a piece with the eye."

"You cut out their eyes?!" Felipe gasps, looking at me like I'm a cannibal alien monster.

"The little spots on the potato skin," I clarify. "That's where the new roots grow. If you cut out those with some of the main potato, in chunks, it grows a whole new plant. But Mom figured out that with Tooba, you don't need an eye. Just the tiniest slice will do. Still, there's a limit."

I walk up to Tooba, where she rests happily in her hydroponic incubator. Mom invented it, a sort of nutrient bath, just liquid, no dirt. The climate is specially controlled, with the temperature and light giving Tooba exactly what makes her happy. Even now a gentle light shines on her. Why not just let her be in the dark when it's night outside? I asked Mom once. "Because outside she'd have starlight," Mom explained. "I want it to be as natural as possible."

"We can't take more than half of her. That makes about two thousand new potato plants. Which is a lot, considering a normal potato can't make more than five or ten. Maybe up to twenty for a super-huge potato. After that, she has to spend a season recovering. She'll regrow to her normal size soon. Then we start all over again."

"Amazing!" Kayla says. "But why do you have to cut her up each year? Can't you start new plants from the potatoes you grow from her? From the kids."

Instantly Felipe pipes up, "Because you can't clone a clone! See! Told you that you can learn all you need to know from science fiction movies!"

I give the exposed part of Tooba a gentle pat, then rotate her so the other side is in the nutrient-rich liquid. I'm glad to see that whatever that flash and boom were, they didn't hurt Tooba. Without her, my family would be ruined.

Of course, we might be ruined even *with* her.

We go back outside. I lock the barn door behind us. Felipe gives a huge yawn. "Let's hurry and see what it is," he says. "I want to go back to sleep." He rubs his eyes and yawns again, so big I can hear his jaw cracking. "It was so cozy in there. What could be better than a sleeping bag, and a tent that smells like French fries?"

I freeze then glance at him, but he's already turned his back to me, looking at the faint glow that's still coming from the far end of the potato field. Even though he's said this kind of thing a thousand times, this time his joke stings a little bit. Why is he making fun of me right now? Do I still actually smell like Lord of the Fries?

I sigh. It's not my fault that I smell like fries. I'm surrounded by them all the time. I spend hours every day cooped up in the back of that stupid Lord of the Fries food truck, cutting potatoes, dunking them in boiling oil, getting burned by the spatters. The smell is in my hair, in my skin. It doesn't come out no matter how much I wash.

I don't want to smell like a walking, talking French fry all the time, and it hurts that he points out that I do.

I remember when Kayla was teaching herself how to build a tractor engine, she smelled like motor oil for a week. And let's not forget how many times Felipe has been covered in toad pee or stinky snake musk from the critters he catches. That's all much worse than smelling like fries—which everyone knows smell delicious.

Not to mention the other smell that someone, I won't say who, was making in the tent while we slept. I don't know what they'd been eating, but believe me, it was no fun being trapped in a tent with *that* smell!

But I don't say anything right now. I just drag behind him and glower at his back, all the while thinking about insult added to injury. Just a few days ago, my horrible neighbor Donnie Webster called me Fry Guy.

Soooo original.

And the really stupid thing is that he's technically a fry guy too.

His father, Rodney Webster, has the farm next door to ours. My family started out being friendly, bringing him and his wife cookies, inviting them over as soon as we'd unpacked. They came over—

exactly once. I remember how Mrs. Webster turned up her nose at all of our furniture, saying snide things like, "Well, it's not to my taste, but I suppose there are *some* who like that sort of thing." Mr. Webster took one bite of the quinoa salad Mom had so lovingly prepared and spit it out. "What are these, bugs? I'm used to a big juicy steak!"

Donnie spent the whole meal secretly kicking me under the table, smiling like an angel whenever I said "ouch."

They never came back again. Probably because we didn't invite them.

Ever since then, there's been a low-grade war between our families. The Websters used to grow onions, but they could never grow sweet ones. They tried to advertise them as "hotter than a Spanish red!" but no one was really interested. People like hot peppers, but mild onions.

Then, just a year after our own potato business picked up, the Websters started growing potatoes too. Theirs are just ordinary potatoes, but we'd already made Solanum famous for fries. They totally jumped on our bandwagon. We did all the work. The Websters reaped all the benefits.

Calling himself the Fry King, Rodney Webster got a shiny red-and-gold food truck that puts our old jalopy to shame. It even has a gold crown with fake jewels welded to the top.

We only have a limited number of our special Tooba potatoes. When we run out, people are still clamoring for fries. So they go and buy from the Fry King. Mr. Webster has a never-ending supply of his perfectly ordinary potatoes. What's more, he has this ridiculous commercial where he's dressed in a purple robe and crown, yelling at people to "Obey the Fry King—Buy My Fries, Peasant!" It makes me feel like throwing up whenever I hear it, but I have to admit, people remember it.

We have quality, small-batch, delicious fries. Literally the best fries on Earth. But not too many of them.

The Fry King has cheap, greasy, tasteless fries by the bucketload, a flashy truck, and really good advertising.

Who do you think is winning this French fry war?

And don't you think little Donnie likes to rub it in my face?

I shake my head, trying to clear my thoughts. There are other things to worry about now.

I open up the fence and we walk carefully between the lush rows of plants.

"Where did it go?" Kayla asks.

"I can't see it," Felipe adds.

I'm taller than both of them, though. When I stand on tiptoe I can just see the unearthly green-blue glow. "Over here," I say, leading the way again. Tonight, at least, I'm not going to worry about middle school, or friendship, or the potato business.

At least, not until Kayla says from behind me, "I'm really glad we're getting to spend this time together before school starts."

That sounds nice, and I'm about to say *me too*, when she goes on.

"When Felipe was over at my house yesterday, my older sister Jeannie was telling us what to watch out for in middle school."

My heart sinks in my chest. I wanted to go over and hang out with them, but guess what? I had to peel freaking potatoes!

"*Everything changes*, my sister said," Kayla goes on. "*Your bodies. Your priorities. But most of all your friends*. She told us that she started sixth grade with two really good friends, girls she'd known since kindergarten. Within a week, one had gotten mad and joined another group, and the other got a boyfriend and didn't have time for anyone else anymore. *Just expect to have a whole new gang of people*, Jeannie said. *Out with the old, in with the new.* I told her that's stupid, because we . . . oh my gosh! Is that . . . ?"

We're close enough to see what's making the glow. It's a . . . something? Smooth, shiny, and metallic, swirling silver and blue and green, the size of a big pumpkin, it is sitting in a little depression, and steaming gently.

"Is it a meteor?" I ask, stepping closer. I reach toward it with one finger.

"Look out!" Felipe shouts, pulling me back and pointing at my feet.

Oozing from the—thing—is a shimmering slime, creeping toward my toes.

CHAPTER 3

SLIME TIME

Like snot from the world's grossest cold, the slime is dripping from the meteor or whatever it is. At first it moves like spilled molasses, just sort of oozing in all directions. But then something strange happens.

After I take a step back, the slime moves slowly toward my feet. But then it stops . . . and changes directions!

This is not possible. There's no hill that it's following. It's not flowing down. It's almost as if . . .

I squat down to watch it more closely. It moves in one direction for a while, then it stops. The front edge quivers, and then it moves left toward me, then right. It acts like a hound dog sniffing the air for a scent, trying to track something.

At last the slime picks a direction and moves sluggishly but relentlessly toward the nearest potato plant. I watch in horror as the ooze envelops the base of the stem. Then . . . it starts to *climb the plant*.

I pick up a piece of mulch from between the rows and try to scrape the slime off. But when I shave along the stem, the slime just moves around the mulch, stretching like bubblegum, and stays clinging to the plant.

Now the ooze is changing. It's starting to bubble. It looks like when Mom makes toffee candy, the butter and sugar gelling together, little bubbles rising slowly. Except it's a shimmery greenish blue, swirling like it is alive. *Traveling* like it's alive. Which is impossible.

Right?

"It has to be a meteor," Felipe says.

"That would explain the sound and the flash," Kayla agrees. "When it entered the atmosphere it broke the sound barrier. That was the big boom."

"And it was probably on fire when it landed," Felipe adds. "That's where the flash came from. Though it isn't hot now." He holds his hand gingerly near the strange thing.

"Careful," I say. "It might be dangerous. Radioactive or something."

"See, I told you I should have brought my telescope. Can you imagine if I'd had it set up when this bad boy crash-landed? And if I got a photo? I'd get my name in *Space Fanatics Weekly*!" He cranes his neck up to the heavens. "I wonder if there are any more. Sometimes meteors are from a debris field the earth passes through. Or it might have been really big but broken up in the atmosphere. I can't believe we found this! Spud, you are so lucky to have this on your property!"

"Do you think we should call the newspaper in the morning?" Kayla asks.

"So super cool!" Felipe goes on, just staring with big rapt eyes at the thing.

"I don't know," I say, answering Kayla's question as Felipe goes into raptures about the thing. He's so excited, I know for a while he'll be content just to talk to himself. "I'm not so sure it is a meteor after all. All the ones I've seen—pictures, I mean—are irregular shapes. And they bump into stuff in space, too, right? Other meteors, space dust? So they get all pitted. This thing is perfectly smooth. It almost looks man-made."

"But man-made things don't fall from space," she says.

"They do if they're secret government experiments," Felipe says, jumping back into the conversation.

"Or," I say significantly, "if they're not man-made at all."

"Huh?" Kayla asks. "You mean if it's woman-made?"

"I mean, what if something *else* made this?" I say in a low, worried voice. "Something that's not . . . human."

We all fall quiet, staring in curiosity and apprehension at this strange thing.

"Okay, let's be sensible about this," Felipe says.

"Scientific," Kayla adds.

"What are the possibilities? One, it is something totally normal that just looks weird. Like . . ." He can't think of any possibilities.

"Er, it's a slow-release fertilizer my parents are trying out?"

"Bingo!" Felipe says. "Wait, is it?"

"No, they would have told me." You should hear our dinner table conversation. Nothing but soil quality and how many worms per square inch good dirt should have, things like that. "Believe me, if there was anything new in the world of potato farming, I would know about it."

"It could be garbage, or something that fell off an airplane," Kayla ventures.

"It could be completely unrelated to the flash and boom," I say. "We could be out here in the middle of the night worrying about nothing."

We all look at each other for a minute, then simultaneously shake our heads and say, "Nah!"

"Okay, then," Felipe goes on, "the only other possibility is that it came from up there." He points to the stars.

"Only because you've been waiting for something to come from *up there* all your life. It could just as easily have burrowed up from underground," Kayla says.

"Oh, like *Mole Men from the Molten Core*!" Felipe says. "An entire civilization of ultra-dense beings who live in the center of the earth."

"You're an ultra-dense being if you think this came from underground," I tease. "There's no sign of digging. It just plopped here."

While we're talking, we're ignoring the goo.

"Oh no!" I smack my forehead when I notice. "Look what it's doing!"

The ooze has spread. Completely bypassing us, it is focusing on the potato plants. Already, almost a dozen of them are covered in that strange bubbling, sizzling slime.

"It almost looks like it's hot, like lava," Felipe says. "See the smoke. Or maybe it's steam."

It's bad enough that this gross stuff is all over the plants, but so far I figured maybe we can come out here in the morning with a hose and wash it all off. If it's burning the plants, though, there's no hope.

We were never rich, but in the first year after Mom discovered Tooba we made enough to pay off the farming equipment, get some new furniture, and put a little bit aside. *For a rainy day*, Mom says. For the first time since we moved, my parents didn't seem worried. Life seemed good. Sure, I worked hard. Probably harder than almost any kid my age in New York state. But I was proud of our special potatoes. And our fries! Man, I could eat them by the bucket load.

We got famous. People came from all over to buy

from the Lord of the Fries. But we were a trend, and trends never last.

I look across our moonlit fields to the Webster property. They have at least three times the land we have. Every inch of it is under cultivation. We like to give our fields time to recover, planting things like alfalfa to give nutrients back to the land. When the circus comes to town we bring home a pickup truck full of elephant poop to fertilize the plots. (Believe me, that's *not* something I'll be talking about in sixth grade.)

We do everything naturally, organically, sustainably, rationally.

The Websters throw money and chemicals at their fields.

And it works. They grow a lot more potatoes than we do. And it looks like soon they'll be making more money, too. People still come for the legendary Lord of the Fries. But more often now they're hipsters who use words like *artisanal* and *gastro-tourism*. Lately, the really long lines are at Fry King.

I had to taste their fries for myself, to see why people were lining up. Of course I couldn't go there personally. Can you imagine if word got out that

Spud the Fry Guy was shopping at the competition? Rodney Webster would probably use it in his next cheesy ad.

So I sent Kayla in disguise. For some reason she decided to disguise herself as a giant banana. ("It was left over from Halloween," she said. "I just meant wear sunglasses and a baseball cap!" I told her.)

She brought us an Xtra Massive Monarch Bucket, and we all tasted them.

"They're, er, salty," Kayla said, smacking her lips.

"They taste like plastic," I said in disgust.

"These aren't even decent dunked in pickle juice!" Felipe said, grossing us all out with his favorite condiment.

But people still flock to the Fry King. We built the reputation. We made Solanum the French fry capital of New York state. But most tourists don't even see our beat-up old camper we converted into a quirky food truck. No, their eyes—and their money—go right to that sparkly new truck with its shiny crown.

Then they taste its subpar fries, go home, and tell all their friends that Solanum's famous fries are completely overrated.

I keep telling Mom and Dad that they need to do

more publicity. "Let people know that Lord of the Fries is the only real fry truck in this town!" I beg them. "Advertise! Network!" I'm not sure what networking is, but I know businesspeople always have to do it.

They just tell me not to worry. "The cream will always rise to the top," Mom says, "and people know quality when they taste it. As long as we have Tooba, we'll survive. This is just a slump."

If this molten lava from outer space burns up all our plants, we won't make any more money this year. That means no money for the mortgage. That means nothing saved for the winter, when baby potatoes are buried under mounds of snow.

That means the end, for this year anyway. As long as we have Tooba we can start again, but honestly, one bad year might be enough to destroy us.

"Is it burning the plants?" I ask, watching the sizzling slime cover another plant. "It doesn't look like it is." The stems are standing strong under the ooze, and the leaves don't look withered. Gathering my courage, I plunge my finger into a churning puddle of goo that's climbing across the mulch.

"Ouch!" I scream, pulling my finger back.

"What happened?" Felipe cries. "Is it acid? Are you mutating?"

"You definitely watch too many science fiction movies. No, it's not acid. I just got a splinter under my fingernail. The goo just feels like . . . goo." I pick the splinter out and look at the slime.

"It's only covering the plants," I point out. "Look—it travels across the dirt and mulch, and leaves a slime trail, but most of it is on the plants themselves."

"Not all the plants," Kayla notices.

I look where she's pointing. Sure enough, there's one little sprout about four inches high that doesn't have any slime on it. In fact, the slime made a clear path around it, surrounding it but not touching it at all.

"That's not a potato. That's a weed I must have missed. The slime only wants the potatoes!"

"How can a slime *want* anything?" Felipe asks. "I mean, it's *slime*!"

"I have no idea. But if this thing is from outer space . . ."

"Maybe it is an alien space probe sent to destroy our agriculture so we starve and then the alien overlords can make us their obedient slaves!" Felipe guesses.

"You sound pretty excited by that idea," I say.

"Well, not the enslavement part. Of course humanity will fight back and win. All it will take to save the day is a young astronomer." He points to himself. "A kid tech genius." He points to Kayla, who smiles proudly. "And a . . . er . . . um . . ."

Go on, say it. A Fry Guy has no part to play in saving the planet.

Kayla saves him. "And the plucky Everyman whom audiences can relate to. You know, like the pig farmer in *Intergalactic Oinkers* who saved the universe."

"Yeah, or the heroic housekeeper in *Evil Dirt from Uranus*," Felipe adds.

"And I know exactly what your movie can be called," Kayla says with a mischievous grin. "*Space Spuds!*"

I groan. At least they're including me, even if it took a stretch.

"But this isn't a movie," I say in despair. "This is real life—*my* real life. And my family's. What if this slime kills the potato crop? What if it keeps spreading and reaches Tooba?" I throw my arms over my head, just like we do in tornado drills. "Aargh! Why did a meteor have to land in my potato field?"

"Er, guys," Kayla says in a voice that sounds both scared and excited. "I'm not so sure it's a meteor."

We stare at the round thing. It's quivering like an egg about to hatch.

Suddenly there's a puff of smoke, a whooshing sound . . . and a door opens in the side of the thing that is most definitely not a meteor.

Then something rolls out of it and lands in the slimy mulch at our feet.

Something small and pale green and chubby.

And . . . alive?

CHAPTER 4

SPACE BLOB

"I think it's dead," Kayla says.

"I'm not even sure it was *ever* alive." Felipe says. "It looks kind of like a vegetable."

"*Maverick Melons from Mars.*" Kayla giggles.

"Melons are fruits."

"Whatever. *Renegade Rutabagas from Regulus.* Better?"

While they banter, referencing all the movies they've seen together, without me, I look at the little alien thing. Because whether it is in fact a living creature, it's definitely not from around here. And that makes it alien.

It's small, almost exactly the same size as the thing we thought was a meteor but which is now obviously a spaceship. If you'd asked me what kind of alien might come out of a spaceship the size of a watermelon I would have guessed a swarm of tiny mouse-sized organisms. Or maybe scurrying beetles.

But this thing must have taken up all available room inside the spaceship. In fact, I can see the imprints of what look like controls, buttons, and levers pressed into his body.

So maybe this isn't an alien after all. Maybe it is . . . packing material?

It's a pale jade green, kind of translucent and wet looking. Sort of like a peeled cucumber. But when I tentatively touch it, it feels more like a gummy bear.

No, I'm sure it is alive. Or was. Right now it's not moving. But its skin feels warm, and somehow I'm certain it's a living thing, not insulation.

I can't see any features on it, though. No eyes or mouth. There are things on the sides that might be arms or legs—or flippers or tentacles—but they are squished into the thing's body. On one end there's a metal device clamped onto its body.

It's not moving at all. As far as I can tell it's not breathing.

Do aliens breathe? Maybe our atmosphere is poisonous to it.

Poor little guy. Imagine traveling all the way through the cosmos on some exciting intergalactic mission of exploration, seeing nebulas and black holes and who knows what other wonders . . . only to crash-land in a potato field in the middle of nowhere, all alone with none of your best friends by your side—or maybe they were by your side but were too busy cracking inside jokes to notice you crashed. I know the feeling all too well.

"Welcome to the club, buddy," I whisper to the alien.

Felipe and Kayla don't notice. They're saying the word "alien" one after the other in increasingly high-pitched voices, until they're both just squealing stupidly.

My friends might be right next to me, but I feel as lonely as this alien must feel, billions of miles from home. Do his friends miss him? I wonder. Will they ever know what happened to him?

I was only six when my family and I moved from New York City. I don't have too many memories of the place. There was a nice park with squirrels and pigeons and a really cool twisty slide. There was an ice cream shop with peanut-butter-and-jelly-bean ice cream. In my memory, the streets were filled with vendors selling hot dogs out of carts.

Mostly I remember the people. Masses and masses of people. I would walk down the broad, crowded streets while traffic roared and honked next to us, between Mom and Dad. They'd each hold one of my hands, and whenever we came to a grate in the sidewalk they'd swing me over. I thought monsters lived down there. But the thrill of being swung was worth any fear.

So many people! So many exciting strangers just waiting to meet you!

Not like here. Here in small-town Solanum, I knew almost everyone within the first year of living here. I might not know them to talk to, but I know them by sight. We all shop in the same Super Mart, the same Dollar Diva.

A chill runs down my spine, and I start to worry. What will happen if Felipe and Kayla don't like me once we start middle school? I feel like it's starting already. Even tonight, with the most exciting and interesting and scary and wonderful event of our lives happening—a real bonding moment—they only want to joke with each other.

If I don't have them, I probably won't have any friends. There was no one else in our elementary school whom I ever got close to. I'm casually friendly with a lot of people, but from the start it was always Felipe and Kayla. There's no one to fall back on.

Sure, once I'm in middle school I'll meet new people. The elementary schools from the neighboring towns of Murphy and Erdapfel feed into our middle school. But what are the odds that someone's going to want to be friends with some random kid who smells like fries?

Thinking all this really makes me sympathize with the squishy green alien at my feet. How long was it in space all alone? Does it need a friend?

Which is all a moot point, because so far it still hasn't moved.

"Please don't be dead," I whisper to it.

Then I notice: it might not be moving, exactly, but it is . . . expanding?

The imprints of buttons and levers that had been pressed on its body are smoothing out. Very slowly, slow as watching grass grow or paint dry, its body is plumping.

Now the little flaps that had been pressed against its skin—the things I thought might be arms or tentacles—are stretching. Then, with an almost inaudible pop, one of them separates from the round body. It looks like a leg and a foot.

As I watch, three more limbs separate. Two legs, two arms. Then two more things pop up from what I'm guessing is its head. Ears? Or maybe antennae?

I'm still not sure if it is alive. After all, a lizard's tail will keep twitching after it falls off.

My friends haven't noticed. They're too busy joking around, speculating which movie this alien is most like.

Sometimes I wish I still lived in New York City. Mom and Dad always talk about it like it was a prison they're glad they escaped from. "It was like a sewer," Mom said. "All smog and dirt and crime." She's glad to be upstate, where the air is pure and clean, where everyone knows their neighbors and people leave their doors unlocked.

Dad agrees with her. "And the people were the worst," he said. He worked for a big corporation.

When I asked him what his job was he just said *a cog in the machine*. "You can't trust anyone there. They seem like your friend, and then *bam*! Everything changes."

I'm starting to think that might be the same everywhere. New York City or Small Town USA—people are still people. Maybe even the ones you trust will let you down.

If the potato business fails, maybe we'll move back to New York City. In a place with more than eight million people, surely I can find new best friends. Instead of living on a farm that's five miles from town, we'd probably live in a crowded apartment building. Think of all the next-door neighbors!

Now, all I have is Donnie Webster. I don't think I'm important enough to have an arch-enemy, but if I was, he'd be it.

But I don't want to move to New York City! There might be some downsides, but for the most part I love it here in the countryside. I love the forests and the hills, the way deer will wander down Main Street. I love the way the snow melts every spring to reveal the crocuses hiding beneath. I love the first breath of autumn that smells like apples and bonfires. I love the creeks and snakes, the rocks and bugs, and all the wonderful adventures to have with the Adventure Bag. I wouldn't have any of those things in the big city.

And I don't want new best friends! Kayla and Felipe are perfect. At least, most of the time. Felipe is so bold and adventurous. He pushes me to do things I'd never dare on my own. And Kayla is so smart and funny. She pretends to be all serious sometimes, but she's really a big goofball.

But we're about to be thrust into this alien world called middle school where we don't know any of the rules. How can I navigate that alone?

I just want everything to stay the same.

The alien in front of me seems to have finished expanding. I still don't see anything like a face, no holes that might be eyes or a mouth. And it's still not moving or breathing.

"Do you think there's anything we can do for it?" I ask. "We could take it to the doctor. Or maybe a veterinarian?"

"Kayla, do you remember that scene from *Star Captain Steve and the Catatonic Cats*?" Felipe asks, ignoring my question. "Those alien cats came to

Earth and they all looked like they were sleeping, and people thought they were so cute they took them home and put them in baskets. Then they all woke up and ate people's eyeballs!"

"Ew, yeah, that's the one I couldn't watch. Gross!"

"Guys, pay attention!" I say, annoyed. "This isn't a movie, this is real life. We have to figure out—"

"You're such a chicken," Felipe teases her. "What's wrong with an alien eyeball-eating cat? It's not like *Space Spiders*, the one where spider venom dissolved people from the inside."

"WILL YOU TWO SHUT UP ABOUT YOUR STUPID MOVIES AND LISTEN!" I shout.

They stare at me, dumbfounded, with their mouths hanging open.

"Hey, we were just . . ." Felipe begins, but I cut him off.

"I get it, you two have seen all the science fiction movies in the world and I haven't. Oh, look at Spud, what a loser, he can't spend fifteen hours a day staring at B movies because he has to work. Well, I'm sick of it! We have a real live alien right here, and you two are talking about movies."

"You need to lighten up, Spud," Kayla says. She

sounds defensive, but I can see the hurt in her eyes. She's never seen me mad like this.

"Yeah, Spud. We didn't mean anything by it. We just . . . really love movies about space aliens."

My face burns hot with shame. My friends didn't meant to hurt my feelings, but I meant to hurt them with my outburst. What kind of friend am I? At this rate I'm going to drive them away with my own bad behavior. These are my friends—my *best* friends. So what if they have their own private jokes? They like me. They're not going to change overnight. No matter what Kayla's sister says.

I need to apologize. "Look, guys, I'm really—"

But before I can get out the word "sorry" we hear a tiny rustle.

"What was that?" Kayla asks.

"Did it just move?" I wonder. I give it a gentle poke. Nothing.

I nudge it a little harder and it rolls over.

"Oh, there are the eyes!" So all this time we'd been looking at its butt.

It has two eyes, shut tight, and a mouth, hanging slightly open. Drooling. Just like I do when I'm super tired. (I never said that, and you didn't hear it!)

In utter silence we stare at the little green entity, watching intently, waiting.

Finally, a few minutes later, its leg gives the smallest twitch.

"It's alive!" I shout, pumping my fist in the air.

CHAPTER 5

SQUISHY GREEN THING

"Shh!" Kayla says, jerking her thumb over her shoulder toward my house. "You said you didn't want to wake your parents up."

"It's alive!" I whisper in the tiniest voice I can manage, looking back toward my house, an old wooden two-story with a wraparound porch on the first floor. It's completely dark. Not even the porch light is on. The first night we moved here Mom left it on, and the next morning there were so many dead moths with burned wings underneath it that she started to cry. After that, we never leave the outside lights on all night.

"What is it, though?" Kayla asks.

"Well, it might be a *Gelatinous Goober from*

Planet—" Felipe breaks off, looking sheepish. "Er, sorry. Force of habit. What I mean is, I have no idea."

"It's definitely an alien life-form, though," I say decisively. "And it fell in my backyard! Can you believe it? This is the most exciting thing to happen in . . . ever!"

All of the awkwardness of our little spat is forgotten in this wonderful new development. "We have to be the luckiest kids in the universe!" I gush.

"Yeah, unless it eats us when it wakes up. Or spits lava."

"Not very likely," I say, rubbing my sleepy eyes.

"Or it could be carrying some deadly disease and wipe out all of humanity. Maybe you shouldn't have touched it without gloves." She looks at what I'm doing. "And you definitely shouldn't be rubbing its extraterrestrial germs in your eyes."

I blink hard. Oh well, too late now.

"Seriously, science fiction movies aside, what do you guys know about aliens? Felipe, you know more about space than anyone. You've been looking at stars with your telescope all your life, and there's not a book on astronomy you haven't memorized."

I turn to Kayla. "And you, you know all about physics and engineering, so you're the one of us who is going to understand how this ship works. And who knows what other kinds of technology it might have? So between the two of you—without quoting movies—what do you think of all this?"

"Well," Felipe says hesitantly, "people have been looking up for hundreds of years. There are legends about aliens coming to Earth. You know—conspiracy theories, Area 51—things like that. But no one has ever actually seen one. There's no photographic evidence. No one ever met an alien. So I always figured either there aren't any . . . or they're just too smart to be caught."

I look at the little blob at our feet. "Figures we'd get the only alien dumb enough to crash."

"What I'm curious about is the spaceship," Kayla says, picking her way around the alien, and the slime, for a closer look. "It's so small! I always thought a ship would have to be massive to withstand the pressures of outer space. Walls ten meters thick. Vessels the size of cities. How on earth does this tiny thing not get crushed in the vacuum of space?"

She tries to peer into the hatch, which is still hanging open. "I wish I could get inside it. Spud, do you have a flashlight?"

I dig into the Adventure Bag and ask, "D-cell, lantern, or mini LED?" I told you we come prepared for adventure.

"Mini LED, please," she says, holding her hand out without looking, like a surgeon preparing to dig into a chest cavity. I slap the flashlight into her palm and she squirms and wiggles until she can get her head inside the ship.

"Darn it, once my head's in I can't fit the flashlight!" she says. "And from out here I can hardly see in. Ugh. I can't see any screens or displays, though there are buttons. How does that thing navigate? It probably can't even turn around in there."

It feels wrong to call our alien friend a *thing*. It was fine when we thought the creature might be a vegetable or some weird kind of alien bubble wrap. But now that we know it's a real, living, breathing creature, we should treat it with more dignity.

(Well, maybe not *breathing*. I still can't see its chest moving. Does it breathe? For all I know that drooling hole I think is its mouth might be another orifice entirely. It might even be the exact opposite of a mouth. Ew!)

I can't stop staring at it in fascination and I realize how adorable this little alien creature is. It's so round and squishy, like a pug puppy. A hairless green pug puppy! I wish it would wake up. The small signs of life its showing—no more than a twitch now and then—are reassuring. But it might be hurt. Maybe even badly hurt. After all, it just suffered a catastrophic crash through Earth's atmosphere.

I won't feel really secure about its health until it wakes up and tells me it is okay.

Then I have to laugh at myself. Do I think it will speak English? I must not be thinking clearly. That's what happens if I don't get enough sleep. Now, woken up so abruptly in the wee hours of the morning, maybe my brain isn't functioning like it should.

Felipe and Kayla are still exchanging theories behind me. At least they're not talking about movies anymore. Now it's all science, big words that I don't really understand. I still feel a little excluded, but I try not to let it bother me.

"Why are you all alone, little guy?" I whisper to the alien. "Or girl, or . . . whatever."

On impulse I scoop it up—it weighs about as much as a cat—and put it on my lap. The creature sighs in its sleep. I see its eyelids twitch.

"If you're on a mission to explore deep space, why aren't there any other aliens with you, huh?" I ask it. I remember reading that people in a coma can still hear and understand words even if they're unconscious. So I figure that it might be comforting to this lost little alien just to hear my voice, even if it isn't awake.

Though for all I know I might sound like a screaming monster to the alien!

"At least I know you didn't come to conquer my planet," I tell it. "You'd have a bunch of soldiers with you. Or are you so powerful you can take over Earth all by yourself?"

It certainly doesn't look powerful. It just looks squishy.

And tired. So tired. At the end of a long day of harvesting, scrubbing, peeling, slicing, frying, and selling potatoes, Mom sometimes uses this expression that really gets to me. "I'm bone-tired," she'll say as she pulls the flowered kerchief off her hair and gets ready to collapse into bed.

Bone-tired. That's how I feel most nights. Like the weariness isn't just skin deep. It isn't even muscle deep, like I've just worked out or run too hard.

No, this tiredness is so profound that it has sunk into my bones, become a part of me.

That's how this alien looks. Bone-tired.

Even though I'm pretty sure it doesn't have any bones in its squishy body.

"But what do you have to be tired about, huh?" I ask it. "Do you have to peel space potatoes all day? Bet you don't."

I sigh, just like the creature did in its sleep.

"No, I bet you're a carefree adventuring alien with the whole galaxy as your playground. I can't imagine how wonderful that would be." Just think of the freedom! To be able to hop into your own personal spaceship and cavort through the universe.

But there's something about the alien that makes me sad. Something I can't put my finger on. As much as I try to imagine it as an intergalactic explorer, bold and free, I can't help thinking it looks lonely and scared. Even in its sleep, it seems deeply worried about something.

"You and me both, bro," I tell it.

Suddenly, the alien's face twitches. Its eyelids flutter.

The alien's eyes are open!

It blinks a few times, long, heavy blinks as if just lifting its eyelids is too much effort. Then, finally, it opens its eyes all the way and focuses on me.

I open my mouth to call my friends—still excitedly speculating, both looking at the ship now—but stop myself. I don't want to scare the alien by shouting. Instead, I turn back to the alien.

"Hi," I say quietly, and smile.

The alien stretches its mouth. Is that a smile? Is it actually smiling back at me?

At this, my grin becomes huge, and the alien kind of cringes away. Of course! It thinks I'm baring my teeth. I laugh. All this time I was thinking about the alien being dangerous to us. It never occurred to me that it might think we're the dangerous ones. Imagine waking up after a crash to find something ten times your size baring its big white teeth at you!

"It's okay," I say. "I won't hurt you. You're safe."

The piece of metal strapped around its head shoots out a spark, making us both flinch. Then the alien's eyes flutter closed. Its body goes slack. I think it passed out again.

"Hey, Spud," Felipe says suddenly. "I think we may be in deep trouble. Look!"

I follow his gaze and see a light on upstairs in my house. In my parents' bedroom.

"Oh no!" I gasp. "We have to get out of here!"

CHAPTER 6

SMART GOO

"We should leave the alien and the ship here and get back to the tent as fast as we can," Felipe suggests. "That way if they come out and check on us we can pretend to be asleep. Then once they're gone we can come back to the crash site."

"No way am I leaving all this alien tech behind!" Kayla says, grabbing little bits of metal scattered around the spot where the alien was lying. I think they're broken parts of whatever that thing is around its head.

"And we can't leave the creature," I say. "What if it wakes up again and it's all alone? It'll be scared. It could wander to the road, get hit by a car. Or even worse!"

"What would be worse than that?" Felipe asks.

"My neighbor Donnie might find him. I've seen that guy throwing rocks at cats. He's a terrible person. If he found an alien he'd probably turn it into a personal servant, or sell it on eBay or something."

Worst of all, I think but don't say, he'd have one more thing to lord over me. Not only does his family have all the money and potato fame now, but he also has my alien? No way will I let that happen.

"Okay," Felipe says. "I've got the Adventure Bag, you get the alien, and . . . I guess we all pitch in and lift the spaceship? How heavy is it?"

We both laugh when we see Kayla pick it up with one hand. "Light as your papier-mâché universe, Felipe." In fourth grade Felipe went a little crazy with an assignment to construct a replica of the solar system. Now his room is filled with papier-mâché planets: huge, colorful, and lightweight, suspended from his ceiling. They're so big and hang so low that walking through his room is like maneuvering through an obstacle course.

That just leaves me. I throw the alien over my shoulder like a sack of potatoes (though much lighter and squishier) and we run back toward the tent.

My feet go *squash-squelch, squash-squelch* as I run. With each step I sink into a few inches of the slime that leaked from the spaceship. The goo! It's spreading!

In the moonlight I can't tell how far, though. It definitely made it at least a few rows away from the crash site, though. How is that even possible? That puny spaceship couldn't hold enough slime to cover more than a few square feet of ground. Especially if the alien was squeezed in there too.

Then I stop dead in the middle of the slimy potato plants.

This isn't goo that was simply brought from space and dumped from a tanker. This started out as a small sample, but it is growing. Not just spreading, but actively growing! The slime is reproducing itself!

Smart, growing, living slime that has already covered a good portion of our potato fields? I'm sure Felipe has seen a science fiction movie like this, but for me it's definitely a horror movie. Mom and Dad are going to kill me! No, worse than that. They're going to be disappointed in me.

I fling open the fence and slam it shut behind me

once my friends are through. For a second I feel relief, like those people in monster movies who escape the killer mutant crocodile in the campground lake . . . but then sit *right on the shore* thinking how lucky they are that they escaped. Mutant crocodiles can go on land, I want to shout to them. But do they listen? Never.

(Okay, so I've watched a few bad movies myself. I just don't talk about it all the time.)

Now I feel like I've done something, just because I've shut the gate. But it's a chain-link fence, designed to keep rabbits and woodchucks and deer out. Not slime. *Idiot*, I tell myself. *The slime can go right through the fence.*

But for some reason, it doesn't. Not while I'm watching, anyway. I see a patch of ooze churn and heave to within inches of the fence . . . and then turn around and slither over another potato plant.

It's only interested in the potatoes.

I glance up at the house, and see another light go on. It's the bathroom light next to Mom and Dad's room. I envision them woken by a strange noise.

"Honey, I heard something!" Mom would say, tugging the sleep mask off her eyes.

“S’nothing,” Dad would say groggily. “Bats in the attic.”

“No, I definitely heard a voice. What if it’s an intruder?”

“What are they going to steal? The food truck? No one but me knows the trick to getting that old engine started. Lord of the Fries is safe, dear. Go back to sleep.”

“But what if it’s Spud and his friends? They could be in trouble!”

This will be enough to make Dad roll out of bed. But first, before he comes to check on us, he’ll splash water on his face. That’s the light in the bathroom, I’m sure of it.

“Hurry, he’ll be out any second!” I hiss to Felipe and Kayla. We rush by the barn, and I just have time to assure myself that the slime isn’t actually at the door. But what if it is creeping around the back? What if it is coming closer and I just can’t see it in the darkness? I watched the slime bury itself in the ground to get at the tubers in the field. What if the goo is launching a surprise attack, traveling underground to sneak up on poor, defenseless Tooba?

But there’s no time to check now. Like a baseball

player sliding home, I dive into the tent and I zip it up behind us.

"Get into the sleeping bags," Kayla whispers frantically.

"There's no time," I say in a muffled voice. I hear the faint sound of the front door opening, then slamming shut when the wind catches it. "Besides, even if we're in our bags pretending to be asleep there's no way he won't see the spaceship. That's too big to hide. We just have to hope he doesn't look in."

"But what if we just . . ." Felipe begins, but I can hear footsteps getting closer. Luckily Dad is walking along a gravel path, so each footfall makes a crunching sound that's distinct in the quiet night.

"Shh!" I caution him. I can hear Dad clear his throat.

He's still only halfway to the tent when he calls out softly, "Spud? Are you guys okay?"

We lie in the dark tent, tense with anticipation. Should I answer? That will just let him know I'm awake already, since his voice wasn't loud enough to wake me up if I was asleep like we're supposed to be. So I stay perfectly still, even when he comes closer.

If he looks inside, we're toast—dropped butter

side down. If the moon is bright enough for him to see the shining slime on the potato fields, we're done for. Luckily the spaceship stopped glowing, but if he looks inside there's no way he won't see it.

And of course our little green friend is sprawled on its back next to me. Maybe we could pass the spaceship off as one of Felipe's extravagant papier-mâché projects. But there's no fib that can cover up an actual alien.

Dad comes a little closer and clears his throat. "Spud? Sampson? Everything good?"

Just then the unconscious alien lets out a weird snort. A *loud* wet snort.

I clap my hand over its mouth . . . then think better of it. After all, the creature doesn't have any nose, so if I'm covering its mouth it can't breathe. Unless it breathes through its skin or something.

I'm trembling, sure Dad will unzip the tent and peer in. I hold my breath . . .

But then I hear him say, "Snoring away." He chuckles. "Not a care in the world, lucky kids. No one woke *them* up to send them on a wild-goose chase." He heads back to the house, calling softly over his shoulder, "Sweet dreams."

I think I don't breathe again until I hear the front door close.

"Sheesh, that was a close one!" I say.

We stay still and quiet for another few minutes. Finally I feel brave enough to peek out. Sure enough, the house is dark again. We give it five more minutes, then turn on the battery-powered lantern to examine our alien and its tech.

Kayla, of course, heads right to the spaceship again. With her mini light she's doing her best to see its electronic innards. "Oh, I think I found the flight controls. There's some kind of writing. The letters don't make sense, but the numbers operate on a pretty simple binary code of . . ."

I start to tune out here. I really admire her intelligence, but once she completely nerds out there's only so far I can follow her. She'll use words like *matrix* and *vector*, and as far as I can understand she might be making the whole thing up.

I get decent grades in math, but when I go to college someday I'll probably take a class Mom told me she took: Math for Poets. Interesting ideas about spirals, not much actual math.

Kayla's happy, but for some reason Felipe is

hunkered in a corner, rocking slightly. He looks like he's in shock.

"Are you okay?" I ask him.

He nods, but continues his rocking. "Just . . . overwhelmed."

Well, that's a first. This is a guy who will jump his bike over a ditch and only realize it's six feet across after he's crashed into the tadpole-filled water below. Felipe's like a cat—he'll climb giant trees, all the way to the canopy, and only then realize that coming down is a lot harder. But it never bothers him. He takes accidents, injuries, surprises, and danger as if they are a part of everyday life. For him, they are.

But somehow this excitement—an alien—is a shock to his system. I know he's going to be fine in a few minutes. For right now, I'm amazed, and kind of proud, that I'm handling this strange situation better than he is. If anyone looked at us now, I'd be the calm one. The guy who has a little green alien on his lap every day of the week.

"I think there might be a maintenance hatch on the bottom," Kayla says, talking mostly to herself. "Ew, there's slime all over the bottom. I wonder if the goo is some kind of fuel? Or maybe a food source?

Or I know! Probably it's a stasis gel. You know how long space travel would take. There's a theory that any space-faring species would have to basically put itself in a coma to travel to another planet, but I don't know if I believe that. Felipe, what do you think?"

Felipe blinks heavily, and slowly comes out of his own stasis. Soon he's taking part in her speculations again, but he still looks like he can't believe any of this. Kayla babbles on like she just drank three cups of coffee. (That's another middle school worry. Kayla's sister says the only way to get through a day of middle school is to drink black coffee in the morning. And I hate coffee! Why is change so hard?)

Now that Dad is back inside and both of my parents are probably asleep, I really should go back out and check on Tooba. It's bad enough that the plants are covered in slime, but I can't let anything happen to her. If she's in danger, I'll have to wake Mom and Dad, no matter what the consequences. She's just too important to risk.

"I'm going to run out to the barn," I tell my friends, and scoop the alien off my lap so I can go. Before I can stand up, two things happen at once.

Kayla, forgetting that her hands are covered in

alien slime, licks her finger to wipe away some spacedust from a label she's found on the underside of the spaceship. I see her eyes go wide in shock as she realizes she might have just poisoned herself. Then her expression grows puzzled.

"That's weird," she begins. "It's . . ."

At that moment I'm halfway to my feet. Just then, I feel something grab my hand, pulling me back. I hear a groan.

The alien is awake! It's holding my hand, and looking at me with a worried expression that plainly says, *Don't go!*

CHAPTER 7

PLORTING

"Do you think it's dangerous?" I ask as we all crouch over the little alien. I probably should have thought about that before I hauled it into our tent. It doesn't *look* very dangerous. Groggy is more like it. Its chubby green belly is gently jiggling now. Breathing, maybe? But its eyes are heavy, like they can hardy stay open.

"Oh, yeah!" Felipe says—and I guess he's recovered from his shock because now he seems thrilled about it. This is the guy who will pick up any snake he sees and *then* figure out if it is venomous. The one who catches catfish by sticking his hand in a hole and letting a whiskery monster bite him. When I first met him at age seven I thought he was super brave.

Now I know he just gets so excited about discovering new animals that he doesn't take time to think.

"What's that thing on its head, do you suppose?" Kayla wants to know. She pokes at it, more interested in that than in the alien life-form itself. "I think the pieces I found on the ground go with it. It looks broken."

"Maybe just its hat?" I offer as the alien stares back at me. It glances at the others, but seems mostly to be looking at me the whole time.

Felipe scrunches his eyes, thinking. "I guess if you travel through space in a rock you might have weird taste in clothes."

"What clothes?" I ask. "It's pretty much naked."

Pretty much is an understatement. Knee-high and chubby, this alien thing reminds me of the story Mom always tells at my birthday parties—about the time when I was two years old and took off all my clothes and diaper and ran through Central Park. A reporter was there. I made the evening news.

"We can't keep calling it an *it*," I say. "Is it a *he* or a *she*?" It doesn't seem to have any, er . . . parts.

"I'm going to go with *he*," Felipe decides. "But how can we even know? Maybe they don't just have girls and boys. Maybe they have girls and boys and *hertzels* and *glombits*! Maybe they grow like plants. Oh, maybe when they reproduce they just *explode*!" He puffs out his cheeks and makes a big booming sound.

It's so loud it makes the little green alien flinch. He squeezes my hand tighter and looks wildly around the room. Does he want to escape? I squeeze his hand back and try to look reassuring. I wish we could communicate.

"Aww, he has purple eyelashes!" Felipe gushes, leaning closer. "Or maybe they're parasites! Or weapons! I bet his eyes shoot lasers!"

So when it—I mean *he*—suddenly sits up we all jump back. Just in case. Felipe has seen so many alien movies that I kind of trust his judgment.

But he's wrong this time. The little thing just blinks at us blearily with his big purple eyes. No death rays.

Then he opens his mouth. No fangs. No spitting poison. Just two little nubby teeth.

"P . . ."

We all look at each other.

"P-luhh . . ."

"I think it's trying to . . ." I begin.

The alien jumps to its feet and says loudly, "PLORT!"

Then he collapses again, his gelatinous sides heaving.

Kayla starts messing with the alien's "hat." He reaches up to bat her hands away, but his little T-rex arms can't stretch that far, so he just goes cross-eyed trying to see what she's doing. She touches something, and the gizmo goes *blip*. She fiddles with something else and it goes *bloop*.

"Whatever it is, it's not working right," Kayla says. "Maybe if I . . ." She twists a knob, then jumps back as the device sizzles and shoots out a puff of smoke. "Guess not. I have to look at it more closely." She tries to snatch it off the alien's head but he flinches away.

"Plort!" he shouts, flapping his little arms. "Plort plort. Plort. Plort-plort plort! Plortplortplortplort. PLORT!"

"Just hold still and give me a minute," she tells the alien. This time she doesn't try to take it off his head, but keeps messing with it. "I might be able to fix it. I've got the spare parts. I just have to figure out what this thing does first."

“Plort?” the alien seems to calm down after this explanation. But that would mean . . .

She gives up after a minute, though. “I can’t figure it out. Maybe if I had my magnifier, but that’s at home.”

Now that the alien is awake, Felipe can’t contain his excitement. He fires off questions—not at us, but at the alien.

“You *are* from outer space, right? I mean, you weren’t created by a government lab, or mutated after a chemical spill?”

“Plort,” the alien says, and nods.

“What’s your mission? Are you here for scientific exploration? Or to spread a message of intergalactic peace?”

“Plort.”

“Felipe,” I say, “you know there’s no way he can understand, right? I mean, he’s an *alien*. What makes you think he’s going to speak English?”

“You’re right!” Felipe says. “Maybe he speaks Spanish.” He switches to that language and keeps interrogating the alien.

I’m trying not to roll my eyes. Or at least, I’m trying not to let Felipe see that I’m rolling my eyes, which is as good as I can manage now. He's talking to an extraterrestrial like it's the new kid in school.

Felipe ignores me. "Or are you here to conquer Earth?" he asks, back to English again.

"Plort!" the creature says, his purple eyes wide. He flaps his arms and shakes his . . . well, if he had a neck I'd say he shakes his head, but his body is all in one piece, so he just kind of rotates.

Just as if he's saying "no."

But that's impossible.

"I think he knows what we're saying," I gasp.

"Plort," the alien replies, bobbing his body with what I think is a nod.

I decide to test it. "If you know what I'm saying, raise your hands."

He does.

"Wiggle your fingers."

He cocks his head, and looks at his hands. He has more of a flipper with an opposable thumb than actual fingers. Kind of mitten hands.

But he wiggles them.

"This is crazy!" Felipe says. "We have an alien—an actual alien—and he can talk to us!"

"Plort."

"Yeah," I agree, "but all he can say is *plort*."

"Plort," our alien affirms at exactly the same time. It's such a perfect moment that our eyes meet. I laugh, and Plort makes a funny *huf-huf-huf* sound I think is laughter.

"Plort!" the alien and I both shout out at once, and the alien falls over, still *huf-huf-huffing*.

It's like Plort and I have our own inside joke already!

"Well, it's a start," Felipe says. "The first step in human-alien relations. Do you think he wants to open an embassy here? I wonder if we can visit his home world. I figured aliens would breathe sulfur or something, but if he can survive here I bet we'd be okay on his planet. What do you say, Plort? Can we visit you?"

"Is that what we're going to call him?" I ask. "Plort?"

"Well, why not?" Kayla says. "Plort, from Planet Plort, in search of fresh plort for all of his little Plortlings." She stifles a yawn.

It's got to be three or four o'clock, almost morning. This was supposed to be a relaxing, bonding night before the horror show they call middle school starts.

We were supposed to be talking about old times, and making plans for all the new things we can do now that we're officially tweens.

Instead we're here with a blobby alien named Plort.

That's awesome and all—a real live alien! But overshadowing the awesomeness is the calamity Plort brought with him. It's hard to be both super excited and super upset at once. But I'm doing a pretty good job of it.

It couldn't be easy, could it? I couldn't just find a cool alien and make friends with it without also having my family business on the verge of disaster at the same time.

"Plort," I ask him, "why did you have to bring slime?" I keep my voice calm, but I want to scream.

Slime!

Oozing, bubbling, living slime that's traveling over my family's prized potato plants *right now*!

Half of a farmer's life is spent worrying about things eating your crops. Caterpillars and aphids and potato beetles like nothing better than to munch on potatoes. We're an organic farm, so a lot of my summer is spent plucking off caterpillars and letting them go in the woods, or releasing ladybugs to eat the aphids.

Mom and Dad know what they're doing. When gophers attacked our crop, they didn't freak out. They started sprinkling coffee grounds around the fields. "Gophers hate the smell," Mom said, "and the grounds fertilize the dirt." I think the gophers just get too wired on caffeine to remember to eat. And Dad put up nesting boxes for owls. "Nothing an owl likes better than a tasty, tender gopher!" he said.

We have organic sprays for mold, which sometimes gets on the leaves.

But *alien slime*? I don't think there's an environmentally friendly spray for that.

By now, that creeping slime has probably covered the entire crop with its swirling mix of blue-green and silver. Not content with the leaves, it's probably burrowed underground. That voracious alien slime is probably eating all of our potato tubers right now!

"I should tell my parents," I say suddenly.

Both Kayla and Felipe look at me like I'm crazy.

"Tell them what?" Kayla asks. "That we have

a spaceship, and an alien? You know adults can't handle that kind of thing. They'd flip out."

"And you know what would come next," Felipe says grimly. "The army would show up and shoot Plort. Or scientists would want to experiment on him, cut him up into sample specimens."

"Plort! Plortplortplort!"

"Don't worry, Plort, we won't let that happen to you," I tell him. I mean, he might have ruined our life, but I can't let anything bad happen to the little guy.

"I should at least wake them up and tell them about the slime," I protest. "Maybe they can wash it off, or . . . I don't know, maybe there's some bug that will eat it?" My parents have an organic way to deal with everything. If they start fighting the slime sooner rather than later, maybe we can save the potatoes.

Plort blinks once, then his purple eyes close and he slumps forward. He catches himself before he falls, then blinks again sleepily. He looks at me and gives a huge yawn. His mouth opens so wide it seems to take over his whole face. When I look into his mouth I can see down to his insides, weird organs pulsing in his semitransparent jelly-like body.

Yawns are catching, and soon we're all yawning too.

"There's nothing they can do until it's light outside," Kayla says with her usual good sense. "We might as well get a couple of hours of sleep before dawn. In the morning we'll see things more clearly."

"Just like my parents will see a slime-covered field thanks to this overgrown alien gummy bear. This is a disaster!"

"Well, you did say that more interesting things would start happening to us now that we're going into middle school."

"I meant like pimples, and girlfriends, and . . . changes. The kind they talk about in that *Getting to Know Your Tween Body* video they showed us last year."

"If I remember correctly, that video said we're all going to feel like aliens for a few years while we adjust," Kayla says. She pokes our new friend gently in his squishy side. He lets out a sleepy *plort*. "Well, now we're the only middle schoolers with firsthand experience with what an alien feels like. Good night, Spud. Good night Felipe."

She curls into a ball and closes her eyes.

“Good night, Plort,” I whisper to my sleepy alien friend.

“Plort,” he replies softly as his purple eyes close.

I try to sleep, but I just toss and turn and dream about golden potatoes crying salty tears out of all their little potato eyes.

CHAPTER 8

GOTTA GET A MOVE ON

I wake up with my head on the most comfortable pillow ever. The rest of my body aches, and feels like I'm sleeping on a slab of rock. But somehow my head and neck are perfectly cushioned.

I'm bad at waking up. That's another thing that worries me about middle school. It starts at the unholy hour of 8:00, much earlier than elementary school. That means I have to leave home by 7:30 at the latest. *No problem*, you might think. *Just roll out of bed at 7:20, splash some water on your face, and head out the door.*

Well, that might work for you. But you're forgetting two things.

Number one: morning rituals get a lot more

complicated as you get older. Starting Monday I'll have to put on deodorant, apply acne cream, gel my hair up into whatever style the latest YouTuber has . . . or I'll be a social outcast. Plus, according to Kayla's sister, I'll have to drink coffee. So mornings probably take forever for any normal middle schooler.

Number two: I'm not a normal middle schooler. I have a *job*.

Each morning there are chores to do. I have to help my parents out by scrubbing the first batch of potatoes and then peeling at least a bucketful. Then when they are naked and soaking in cold salty water I can start on my other morning chore. Every day, I scrub down the Lord of the Fries food truck, trying to make it look a little less decrepit.

Only then am I free to get myself ready.

I'm going to have to get up at the butt crack of dawn every morning!

Worse yet, Kayla's sister said that around exam time I'll have to pull "all-nighters." I don't think I can handle that! Last night I pulled a "half-nighter" and I'm a mess.

And like I said, getting up is really hard for me. I don't think my brain works first thing in the morning.

It takes me about ten minutes to become fully awake.

At first I feel like I'm still dreaming, but I start to have control over my dreams. My brain is making the transition from random bizarre night dreams to pleasant daydreams. This morning, as I lie in that weird half sleep, I'm thinking about a world without French fries. A glorious planet where no one fries a single tuber slice. When people eat burgers, they don't ask for an extra-large order of anything beside them. The only thing people put ketchup on is their eggs.

Oh, what a beautiful world!

Slowly, this world fades, and I start to become conscious. I hear sounds: first, the whistle and chirp of a chickadee and the low, mournful coo of a dove. My sleepy brain has no idea where I am. Then I hear another sound: other people breathing.

Oh yeah, I think blearily. *I was having a sleepover.*

In sluggish increments my brain pieces things together as I lie on my super-soft pillow with a smile on my face. Life always seems to be pretty great before I've quite woken up.

Then it all comes rushing back to me like a flood. Like a tsunami!

I sit bolt upright and open my eyes. My first glance around the dimly lit tent confirms all my fears. Yup, there's the spaceship.

And that really comfortable pillow I was enjoying so much?

That's Plort.

Everyone is still asleep. Kayla is curled into a tight little ball like an armadillo. Felipe had unzipped his sleeping bag to use it like a blanket. Now he's sprawled on his back, spread out like a starfish.

Plort looks kind of like when I found him, though without the imprints of spaceship controls pressed into his jelly-bean body. His limbs and ears, or antennae, or whatever they are, have all sort of sunken into the rest of his body, turning him into a ball.

His mouth is hanging open, showing two nubby teeth.

And he's drooling.

I feel closer to him already.

If I'd woken up and realized it had all been a dream, that would have made a lot more sense. But here in the early morning light there's no denying it. It's real.

Judging by the light, it can't be much later than six. The sun has only just come up. We've only gotten a few hours of sleep, and I can feel it. My brain is fuzzy, and my mouth feels like there's a hamster living in it. What I need is a big glass of water, a toothbrush . . . and about seven more hours of sleep.

Then my brain wakes up completely and kicks into high gear. There might be a lot of confusing things about this adventure, but one thing is crystal clear. I do *not* want to be here when my parents wake up and find that alien slime all over our potato crop!

"Guys, wake up!" I shout, suddenly frantic. "We have to go."

"Go where?" Kayla mutters sleepily as she uncurls, stretches, and then curls back up in the opposite direction.

That's a good question. Where's the best place to hide an alien and its ship? Luckily Plort isn't that big. But there aren't a whole lot of places where adults don't poke their noses in at least occasionally.

Take my room, for instance. A few weeks ago one of the hinges on my bedroom door succumbed to wood rot. Our house is really old, from the 1920s. Mom calls it a historic landmark. Dad calls it a handyman's nightmare. For a while my door was hanging half off by the last hinge. Then Dad got around to taking the whole thing off.

But fixing it is going to take some serious carpentry, and Dad won't have time until things slow down in the winter. So Mom tacked up one of those hanging bead curtains across my door frame. It looks cool, but doesn't exactly give me much privacy. No one can see in unless they try, but a gentle breeze sets the beads swaying. No way to hide an alien in there.

Felipe has this weird relationship with his parents where they just walk into each other's rooms unannounced. That's going to lead to disaster or psychological scarring one of these days, I'm sure.

As for Kayla, with five kids, her mom, two cats, and a three-legged dog all living in a pretty small house, there's really no way to sneak anything in.

I wrack my brain trying to think of a perfect place. Maybe the woods? The national forest is close by. But what if it rains? And even though there are thousands of acres, someone could still stumble on Plort.

Maybe our cellar? We store potatoes underground in our big, dry basement, but we just use one section of it. The light doesn't reach all the way to the back. Maybe if Plort was really quiet?

But no. There's still a good chance my parents would find him. And I can't stand the thought of leaving Plort alone in a cold, dark cellar with centipedes, spiders, and who knows what else.

If only there was a place close to one of our homes, but where absolutely no one else goes.

Then it hits me.

"Kayla, wake up!"

"Wanna sleep," she murmurs, squeezing her eyes shut.

"No, we have to go. Felipe, get up!" I whip his sleeping bag off him, and with a look of shock he covers himself as if he were naked underneath—even though he's still fully dressed, just like the rest of us.

"Oh, er . . . what?"

"I've figured it out. We have to bring Plort and the ship to Kayla's lab!"

The "lab" is really a dilapidated old shed in the backyard. They have another, newer shed in the opposite corner, mounted on cement, where they keep their lawn mower and tools. But this one is left over from the last homeowner. It is made of rotting wood and sheet metal, and sits on the bare ground. Kayla made the roof and walls watertight with buckets of sealant, but there's nothing she can do about the floor.

Anything that creeps or slithers or crawls can get into Kayla's lab. It doesn't much bother her. "Snakes and beetles have zero interest in electronics," she says. And though she doesn't love toads and snakes and things as much as Felipe and I do, she doesn't mind them either. She's indifferent to anything that doesn't interfere with her tech projects.

Her brothers and sisters are another story. They *hate* creepy-crawlies. They're convinced that if they so much as touch an earthworm they'll die. They think every garter snake is a deadly viper. And bugs? Forget it. They'd rather poke a hornet's nest than go inside of Kayla's shed. As her big sister Jeannie once said, "At least with the hornet's nest you can run. In the shed you're trapped with whatever disgusting thing slithered inside."

Kayla does everything she can to play up the image of her lab as a rat-infested dungeon. She'll draw fake bug bites on her arms with red pen. Every couple of months she'll let a giant millipede loose in the house and say, "Oh, it must have hitched a ride from the lab."

In a crowded, tiny house, her lab is the only real privacy she ever gets. “There's *always* a line for the bathroom,” she told me once. “Always. Even at midnight.”

Also, some of her experiments are so delicate that they'd be destroyed by curious kid hands. Her troublemaking little twin brothers would probably play catch with one of the projects that's going to get Kayla into MIT someday.

(Don't ever ask her about her college plans unless you have an hour or two to spare. She'll regale you with the comparative merits of all the science and technology schools. Right now her top pick is the Massachusetts Institute of Technology, though she says she'd grudgingly accept a full scholarship to Harvard.)

Finally I have Felipe and Kayla more or less conscious. “We don't have a lot of time. My parents will be up any minute, and when they see the slime I'm in big trouble.”

They pack up their things and get ready to go, both complaining about their lack of sleep. “Remember our first sleepover?” Kayla asks Felipe. “We were what, five? And we thought staying up all night was mandatory on a sleepover.”

"We were both hysterical at two a.m., and my mom had to explain to us that we were actually allowed to sleep if we wanted to."

They crack up over this, and I sigh. Another memory I missed out on.

I go to shake Plort awake and find his purple eyes are already open. He's watching the interaction between Kayla and Felipe. Then he looks back at me and gives me a sympathetic *plort*.

Is it weird that I feel like this alien I just met understands me better than my best friends do?

"Plort, it isn't safe here," I tell him.

His eyes get huge and his limbs and ears all pop out of his body with a squelchy sound. "Plort? PLORT???"

"No, not serious danger. Not like space scorpions with laser beams or whatever it is you're used to. Regular danger like Mom and Dad."

"Plort?" he asks, sounding less worried.

"They're going to be crazy mad about all that slime you left on our fields. And if they see you they'll want to do Grown Up, Serious Things."

Like call the police, or the New York Department of Agriculture. Adults always overreact.

"So we're going to take you and your ship to my friend Kayla's house. She has a lab."

"Plort!" he says, shaking his head.

"No, not the dissect-you kind of lab. A fix-your-technology kind of lab. Gee, Plort, we're your friends!"

Plort gives me his two-tooth smile and starts to waddle toward the tent flap.

"No, you can't just walk there. First of all your legs are so tiny that . . ." Plort looks miffed at that. "Sorry. You might have been the tallest in your class on your home world, but here you're just a shrimp. No offense. It would take you hours to walk there. We're going to ride our bikes."

"Plort?"

"Er, things on wheels, they go fast and you can do tricks on them. But we can't let anyone see you. So, uh, you'll have to go in the Adventure Bag."

I hold it open, while he looks inside dubiously. "I'll take some of the gear out," I say, pulling out the towel folded on top. I read somewhere that a towel is the most useful thing to have with you, so we always pack one. So far, though, it just takes up space. We've never used it once.

Reluctantly, Plort crawls inside, settling himself on top of a can of bug spray, a multi-tool, and a bag of granola. He gives a tiny, worried *plort* when I zip him up into the darkness.

We creep out into the pinkish morning light. Saturdays are big for Lord of the Fries, so Mom and Dad will be up any minute getting ready. They promised to give me until nine to hang out with my friends, but after that I'm supposed to help them with the food truck.

"The bikes are by the house," I say, slinging the Adventure Bag over my shoulder. I can feel Plort wriggle against my back. Kayla has improvised a bungee-cord sling to carry the spaceship. "We'll have to walk across the open, and just hope they don't look out their window."

Even though we're in a hurry, I pause a moment to take in the awful sight of our potato fields. They are completely covered in that slimy green-blue ooze. It even seems to be moving in a slow, swirly current. It makes the field look like an underwater garden. The potato plants are still standing, but there's not a single one free of slime.

The only good thing is that it hasn't spread to the

barn. But it's really close. In fact, it looks like it has made it all the way up to the cement foundation the barn is standing on.

Maybe the slime can only spread on organic stuff, like plants and dirt? Whatever the reason, at least Tooba is still safe.

For now.

CHAPTER 9

ESCAPE!

We sneak toward the back of the house, where our bikes are all parked. While we're still on the side of the house I hear the back door open. With a frantic gesture I shoo everyone back. I hear a rustle, and then I see Boopsnoot slither past us. I let out a sigh of relief.

Boopsnoot is a hognose snake, the first that Felipe and I caught together. I kept him as a pet for about a year and he got pretty friendly. Then once Lord of the Fries started I had so much work that I thought I was neglecting him, so I let him go. Now he pretty much lives in the leaf pile behind the stacks of firewood, hunting toads and salamanders. He got so used to me that I can still pick him up without provoking a hognose snake's typical *very* dramatic defense display, but he's still scared of other people.

I'm about to take another step forward when I gasp!

My dad! He's come out to feed the chickens who run half wild around the place. We never bought chickens. They just turned up, and then Rodney Webster next door started accusing us of stealing his chickens. I think they just like us better. Chickens have good taste.

I peek around the corner, watching him. Oh no, he's wearing that stupid short bathrobe. Mom told him never to wear that again. Now he's bending down to pat one of the chickens . . .

Nooooo! I'm being mooned by my dad!

I make a strangled, gargling sound, and Dad stands up and turns around. "Spud, is that you?"

"Go, go, go!" I hiss to the others, and we start to run. "Down here!" I fling open the outside access to the cellar, and we jump down. It's more than a six-foot drop. The trapdoor slams behind us.

"Darned raccoons!" I hear Dad say as he opens the trapdoor.

"Move!" I whisper. "Away from the light." A shaft

of sunlight slants into the dark cellar, and we hunker on the far side by the steps leading up to the house. I can see my dad peering in, but he obviously can't see us.

"You just wait, raccoons!" he shouts with a shake of his fist. "I'll be back—with a broom!" He hurries away, leaving the door open.

"He's going to go around through the house and try to scare the raccoons out. I mean, us!" We run back to the trapdoor. "Oh no! Where's the ladder?" We never go into the cellar this way. Usually there's a bin at the base and we just dump potatoes in from the outside. Then we gather them from the inside entrance to wash and prepare them in the kitchen. There's supposed to be a ladder in here for emergencies. But it's gone.

Then I remember that mom had to change a light bulb in the hallway. The ladder is still upstairs.

Jumping down was easy. Getting out is going to be a problem.

I can reach the top of the trapdoor, but the others can't. "We'll help you up," I tell Felipe. He's the heaviest, but also the strongest. With a foot on Kayla's knee and one on mine, he can pull himself up. We hand up the spaceship. Kayla is light enough for me to boost her up myself.

Now all I have to do is scramble up and we're free to grab our bikes. Mom and Dad will be too focused on the "raccoons" to notice us.

I'm almost all the way up when I hear, *zzzziiip*.

Then my backpack is suddenly lighter.

"No, Plort, what are you doing?" While I swing my legs onto solid ground, he's jumped right out of my backpack. He tucks in his arms and legs and bounces like a green rubber ball halfway across the cellar. Then his limbs shoot out again and he toddles over to where the first-generation potatoes are spread out on layered pallets.

"Plort-plort!" he says excitedly, looking back at me and pointing to the potatoes. Then he picks one up and takes a big bite out of it.

"No, you don't eat them raw . . . Oh, forget that. Get back here! They'll be down any minute!"

Just then I hear the cellar door open, and the sound of the light's chain being pulled. "Dang, it's out again. Honey, can you get the flashlight? I don't want these raccoons to get one single bite of our potatoes."

That buys us a minute. I might just have time to jump down and save Plort.

Now he's ambling back, looking disappointed. "They're much better cooked," I tell him, and prepare to jump down.

But now I hear Mom say, "That's okay, I have one in my pocket from when I went up in the attic this morning." They're coming down! There's no time to rescue Plort. I can already see their feet marching down one step at a time, slowly because like everything in this old house, the stairs are rickety.

That's it. We're doomed. Mom and Dad will see Plort and then . . .

Plort is looking up at me, smiling. Then . . .

He starts bouncing. He's tucked his arms and legs in and is bouncing up and down. Just a few inches at first, but higher each time. A foot. Two feet. Three feet.

"Hold my legs," I whisper to Felipe, and lie on my belly, reaching as far down as I can. On the next bounce I manage to catch Plort in my arms. "You're full of surprises, little guy," I say. Then his arms pop out and he gives me a squishy hug.

"You locked the bikes?" I ask in amazement a

moment later. "We're in the middle of nowhere. Who's going to steal them?"

"Well, you said you didn't trust that kid Donnie who lives next door," Kayla says sheepishly. "Plus I wanted more practice opening a lock."

"Well, this is your chance to do it fast!"

"Stop pressuring me!"

By the time she sets our bikes free, the raccoon crisis is over. I hear the cellar trapdoor slam. "Come around this way," I say as we push our bikes. "If we're lucky, they haven't looked outside yet."

We're not lucky.

"SAMPSON McKINLEY, WHAT IS THE MEANING OF THIS?"

For such tiny woman, Mom sure has a big voice.

"What should we . . ." Felipe begins.

"Don't stop!" I shout as I throw my leg over my bike.

"But what if . . ."

"Don't stop for anything!" I'm pedaling as hard as I can. Felipe is right behind me. Kayla, with the awkward spaceship over one shoulder, is having a harder time.

We race past the Lord of the Fries truck, past the

barn, around the fields until we come to our long gravel driveway. Standing right in the middle is Donnie Webster. His arms are crossed, and he's wearing a bulky backpack.

"Stop right there," he says, like he's the police or something. I skid around him, and for a second I think he's going to grab me. But then Felipe sideswipes him, throwing him off balance, and we all jet past him.

"*Spud!*" I hear my dad bellow as we hit the main road. I don't slow down.

"What was Donnie doing there?" I gasp when I have enough breath to talk. "He hates me. I hate him. There's no reason for him to be coming up our driveway."

Whatever it is, I know it can't be good.

CHAPTER 10

THE LAST POTPOT

The first mile is on a country road, rutted and filled with potholes. It's curvy and not very wide, and cars coming from the other direction sometimes swerve into our lane. So for a few minutes I have to concentrate so hard on not crashing that I can't think about anything else.

Then we hit the main road, smoothly paved with an actual bike lane, and I can calm down enough to ask again, "What the heck was Donnie Webster doing in my driveway?"

"He's your next-door neighbor," Kayla says. "Maybe his mom sent him over to borrow something."

"No way," I say. "If any of those Websters wanted anything they'd probably try to steal it, not borrow it.

Just like they steal our business. Felipe, you saw how he tried to grab me."

"Well . . ." He hesitates. "It *kinda* looked like that."

"You practically crashed into him to save me!" I remind him.

"I just lost my balance after I thought *you* were going to crash into *him*," Felipe says.

"Well, you just lost your Hero of the Week award," I grumble at him.

I know what I saw, though. Donnie tried to stop me as I rode by. Maybe he was just being his usual jerky self. Maybe he had some other reason. But it leaves me with a bad taste in my mouth.

A couple of people give us funny looks as they drive past. At first I think it's because of the spaceship, though for all they know it is just a toy. Then I blush as I realize I still have my pajamas on! Kayla and Felipe slept in comfortable shorts and T-shirts that work just as well for day or night. But I'm wearing pale blue pajamas with a purple stripe.

Could this day get any worse?

Well, yes, because now I have to pedal through town. By the time we get to Kayla's house I'm sweaty and embarrassed.

Kayla's mom is on the front porch, a kerchief tied around her hair, a broom in her hand. A look of quick annoyance flashes over her face as we roll up, but she replaces it with a smile almost instantly. "What are you kids doing here? I thought you'd be at the sleepover at least until nine."

"Sorry, Mom," Kayla says, giving her a kiss.

"Do you maybe want to go to Felipe's house?" she suggests, and Kayla laughs.

"Don't worry, Mom, we'll stay out of your hair. We're going to be in my lab for a while."

Mrs. Jeffers looks positively relieved.

"Have fun, then, kids. Don't blow anything up!"

We know this isn't a joke. "Don't worry, Mom," Kayla assures her. "We're not working with anything combustible." She scrunches her face, pondering. "I think." She waves her hand and we head to the back as Kayla adds for our benefit, "Who knows what might be in the spaceship?"

"Your mom seemed upset that we're here," I comment.

"Well, she works long hours," Kayla explains. "And then me and my sisters and brothers are usually home. So she never gets any time to herself. This morning I know she managed to get rid of all of us at once, and she doesn't go in for her shift at the Dollar Diva until two. So she was hoping to have the morning completely alone."

"If she was looking forward to it, why is she cleaning? Shouldn't she be reading a magazine and eating bonbons or something? Getting a massage or pedicure or whatever it is moms do?"

Kayla rolls her eyes. "Mothers. Who can figure them out? Come on, I just straightened up the lab yesterday. There should be enough room for all of us."

If this is the straightened-up version, the messy version was probably a public health hazard. There are wires everywhere, snaking in and out of hard drives and other computer and phone pieces I can barely recognize. Everything is up on fold-out tables or propped on pieces of plywood to keep it off the ground—which is bare dirt covered with layers of newspaper and a few logs and scraps of metal. There are weird pieces of technology everywhere. It looks like a computer cannibal went to town in a Best Buy, ripping all their stock to shreds and eating half of it.

"See how neat it is?" Kayla beams as she shoves a flashing motherboard aside to put down the spaceship.

"Er, sure," I say, sitting on top of last Sunday's comics page and unslinging my backpack. When I unzip it Plort pokes his head out. "Plort!" he says in slow amazement as he looks around.

"I know, right?" I say to him. "You'll be safe here, and in the meanwhile she might be able to fix that thing on your head."

"It's a communication device, right?" Kayla asks Plort. He nods. "Yeah, I figured that would explain you being able to understand us but us not being able to understand you. The incoming data is translating just fine, but the outgoing data is being jumbled. Can I see it?"

Plort nods, and she takes it off his head.

"Don't worry," I tell him. "Kayla can fix anything on Earth." I realize what I've said and laugh. "Well, probably anything from space, too!"

But this time Plort doesn't give his funny, gurgling laugh. He just looks at me with his head cocked to one side, perplexed. Then he gives a little shrug.

Of course. Without his translator he can't understand me. It's a sad and kind of lonely feeling not to be understood. I feel like even though he's from another planet and I'm an Earthling, Plort and I have so much in common already. He knows what it's like to be on the outside looking in. It's nice to have someone who sympathizes with me. But while our communication is taken away, that's all over.

I watch as Kayla attaches the parts that broke off when Plort tumbled out of his spaceship.

"Well, that was easy enough," she says. "Like plugging in a USB cable. But look, this part has some damage. I'm not sure if the connection is good."

She puts on giant magnifying goggles that make her look even more alien than Plort—like a human bug-eyed frog. "Yup, just as I thought. The wire here is frayed. And this, which is some kind of a data chip, looks compromised. Maybe if I just . . ." She takes out a tiny handheld soldering iron and fuses two parts of the device together. A strange metallic smell fills the lab.

"That might work," she says, putting it back on Plort's head.

"Plort," he says experimentally.

"On the other hand, it might not," she says, snatching it off again. She melts more tiny bits of solder, forming new electronic connections, an intense look on her face. Then she hooks up one of her homemade devices into the translator. It looks like an inside-out phone, and connects with a bright red cord—the kind you'd definitely cut first if it were a bomb about to explode. Now that I think about it, most of Kayla's gizmos look like bombs about to explode.

"This is a little something I've been working on. A diagnostic and repair tool. In theory it should be able to work with anything that processes information." She frowns at the screen, reading indecipherable data. "It doesn't care what the information is, it just finds a more efficient way to transmit it. So it should be able to handle alien technology."

"You are getting into MIT for sure," Felipe says admiringly.

"I wonder what schools are like on Plort's home world," Kayla muses as she works. "Maybe they're even better than MIT. Imagine, being the first human to attend an intergalactic university!"

Finally, she says, "That's all I can think of to try for now. Let's see if it works."

She sets the device gently on Plort's head. Immediately it gives off a flash of blue-green light, which I hope is a good sign. Plort's eyes go wide and he looks at me.

"Ma potpot!" he says urgently, grabbing my shirt. "Ma potpot! Ma potpot!"

I sigh. I guess it didn't work after all.

"Hey, at least he's not just saying *plort* anymore," Felipe says.

"Yeah, but *ma potpot* is just nonsense," I say. "It doesn't mean anything."

But strangely, Plort is nodding enthusiastically. "Ma potpot," he says again, still nodding.

"Can you still understand what I'm saying?" I ask. He nods again. "Well, that's something. But we still can't understand you." I lean back against the corrugated metal wall of the shed, dejected. A beetle crawls over my ankle, but I hardly notice. I really hoped I was going to be able to fully communicate with my new friend.

"Plort," he says, patting my hand reassuringly. I close my eyes, tired and disappointed.

But then . . .

"Last poppot bad Plort bad plortplortplort sorry run space!"

"Huh?" I sit bolt upright, staring Plort right in the eyes. "There were actual words in there."

"Yeah, but nothing that makes sense," Felipe says.

"The translator is still glitching," Kayla says. "It will probably just spit out random words."

"No, I don't think those were completely random. I think the translator is doing its best to translate even though it is broken. Say some more, Plort. Maybe I can understand you."

"Sol gravity so fast Plort slingshot! Zoom!" Plort makes a quick arcing motion with his hand. "Wrong! Mistake! Plort, plort plort!"

Plort is getting more frustrated. There's so much he wants to say but he knows that his words are coming out garbled and confusing. I recognize some of the words, but can't quite figure out what he means. To make matters worse, it sounds like Plort is speaking with a thick accent, half swallowing some of the words.

"Potpot go! Solo potpot. Ma potpot. Go!"

"Potpot?" I repeat. "That's something important?"

"Aye-aye-aye!" he says, nodding and sounding like a deranged pirate.

"It's something you came to Earth for?"

"Aye-aye yup!"

"But what is it?" I ask.

"Ma potpot—MA POTPOT!" he says, jumping up and down.

"Okay, I get that it's something special. Is it another alien, like you? A friend?"

He shakes his head.

"Something like money? Treasure?"

Plort shakes his head. He looks so frustrated, mouth pinched tight. "I'm sorry, Plort, we're doing our best. We'll keep guessing."

But five minutes of guessing later we still haven't figured out what this all-important ma potpot is, and Plort looks like he's about to cry.

"Ma potpot," he says in despair. "Solo potpot in stars."

"Whatever it is, I think it's the last one," I tell the others.

We try a few more guesses, and then Felipe jokes, "Is it a weapon?" He's always ready to think aliens are planning to take over Earth.

To my surprise, Plort smiles and starts jumping up and down. "Fight fight fight! Big fight big Plort!"

We all shrink back to the far corners of the lab and stare at Plort. Plort, who we thought was our friend. Plort, who we were doing everything to help.

"I thought you said you weren't here to conquer Earth," I say softly. "I thought you didn't mean us any harm. We certainly didn't mean you any harm."

"Plort?" he whispers. He looks like he can't believe what I just said. "Plort good. Plort . . . friend."

"But if this ma potpot is a weapon, what are you going to use it for if not to take over Earth?"

Plort gives his squelchy little chuckle and says, "Mycoslime plus potpot equal BIIIGGG Plort! Big strong safe Plort. All the Plorts. All the everywhere Plorts!"

He certainly doesn't look like an enemy of Earth.

"Okay, if this ma potpot isn't a weapon to fight us, who do you have to fight?"

Plort shakes in fear, his green jelly belly rippling in fright. He looks up, pointing, and I can tell he's not pointing at the rusting metal of the shed roof. He's pointing *beyond*.

"Big race," he says. "Hot chase! Big boomboom-boom! Purple! Purple!"

He shakes his head, knowing that his words aren't coming out right.

"Big purple come," he says at last in a small, scared voice. "Big purple . . . big Tantrunium. End Plort. End everywhere Plorts."

"Something is chasing you?" I ask in alarm.

Plort nods, looking terrified now.

"Look, whatever's after you, you're safe here," I tell him. Plort looks dubious. "I mean it. We're going to do everything possible to protect you. We'll help you find your ma potpot. We'll keep you safe from the Big Purple."

"Plort?" he asks wonderingly. "Not your Plort. Not your Big Purple."

"That doesn't matter," I tell him. "I'm your friend. We're all your friends. That means your problems are my problems. That's just what friends *do*."

Plort sighs and closes his eyes. Poor little guy. He's so tired, so scared.

"This thing chasing you, does it know you're here on Earth?" I ask him.

Plort nods.

I swallow hard, trying to be brave for Plort's sake. "Is it close?"

Plort squeaks. His lips tremble. "Almost. Here."

Then the translator shoots out a shower of sparks, and our alien friend goes back to saying nothing but *plort plort plort*. . . .

CHAPTER 11

BUSTED

Kayla gets the translator working a little bit again after its latest breakdown, but Plort can only say a few words of English, and in such a weird and roundabout way that Felipe and Kayla find him almost impossible to understand. I can usually tell more or less what he's trying to say, even if there's a lot of guessing, too.

The more I listen, the better I am at deciphering his words. We're really forming a connection.

In fact, the closer Plort and I become, the closer Felipe and Kayla seem to get. They're huddled together over the spaceship right now. I can hear them using their own private language—words like *G-force* and *tilt* and *yaw* and *vectors*. Things I kind of know are actual words, but are still pretty much gibberish to me. I can understand Plort with his broken translator better than I can understand my best friends right now.

“Sorry to interrupt your very important conversation,” I say. “But we’ve got actual problems here.”

Kayla looks up at me sharply. “What do you mean? Understanding this spaceship is super important. It got damaged in the crash, so if Plort ever wants to get home again we have to figure out how to fix it.”

“Yeah, eventually,” I say. “Right now there are more pressing matters to worry about. There’s an actual invading alien chasing our friend, and he might be here any moment.”

I have no idea what this Big Purple, or Tantrunium, or whatever it is might actually be like. For all I know it is a mean purple version of Plort, which shouldn’t be too hard to handle. I’ll just stuff him in a garbage can or something and Plort can haul him off to intergalactic prison.

But something about Plort’s level of terror tells me that this Tantrunium has to be some kind of giant deadly monster. All those stories Felipe keeps telling? The movies about aliens with fangs and laser beam eyes, spitting poison and enslaving the earth? I'm betting that's what Tantrunium is like.

"But what are we going to do about that?" Felipe asks.

I shrug. "Haven't figured that one out yet. I guess we help him get his ma potpot first. Then maybe he can defeat this Tantrunium guy on his own."

Felipe bites his lip. "Er, Spud? Can I talk to you outside for a minute?" He glances meaningfully at Plort. "Privately. You come too, Kayla."

Reluctantly she leaves the spaceship, and we go outside.

"Plort?" the little alien questions.

"We'll just be a minute," I assure him.

Outside, though, I'm not so cool. "You know, that's really rude of you. Anything you can say to me you can say in front of Plort. We're all in this together. How do you think he feels being left in there all alone while we're out here talking?"

"Well," Felipe says, "I kinda wanted to talk about *him*."

"Yeah, I figured. Which makes it even more rude." I cross my arms and tap my foot. "So, what do you have to say about Plort?"

Looking nervous, Felipe says, "How do you know he's our friend?"

"Because he . . ." I start. Then I stop. Because he's small and scared and interesting and hasn't done anything bad yet. Except . . .

"What about the slime?" Felipe asks, reading my mind. "That stuff is alive! An invasive alien life-form. And it covered all of your potatoes overnight. What if it spreads to the rest of the world's crops? The whole planet might starve."

"Plort would never . . ."

"How do you know? Maybe they send their cutest, smallest, most innocent-looking alien to trick us. We might actually be helping him take over Earth!"

"No, that's not true," I insist, but Felipe's making sense. Am I being played by an adorable alien?

"How can you know? I mean, he seems really nice, but we can hardly communicate with him. All we know is he's looking for a *weapon*, for goodness' sake. And that someone is after him. What if he's actually a criminal? What is he stole a super weapon and he's trying to take over the *whole universe*? What if this Tantrunium is the chief detective trying to bring in a wanted fugitive?"

"I can't believe that Plort could be a bad guy," I say, but my voice is shaky.

"I'm not saying he is," Felipe admits. "In fact, I don't really think he is. But the point is *we don't know*! I just want you to keep your guard up. Be on the alert for any signs that he's dangerous, or going to betray us."

"I feel like we're betraying him talking like this."

"Okay, I won't say anything else, 'cause you're probably right," Felipe concedes. "But I just had to say something. I can tell how much you like him, how involved you're getting."

"Aren't you both pretty deeply involved too?" I ask.

"Well, yeah, but . . ."

"Fine, then. We work together and help Plort find his ma potpot, and keep him safe. Agreed?"

I stalk back inside before they can answer. Behind me I hear Kayla say, "Gee, what's gotten into him lately?"

Felipe shrugs.

Once we're settled back inside Plort gives me a worried look. "Plort good?"

I look at his chubby, gummy-bear body, his big innocent purple eyes, and I have to say, "Yeah, you're good, buddy."

Plort sighs, and in a little while his eyes start to close. *Good idea*, I think. Maybe once I've caught up on a couple of hours of sleep I'll be able to figure out what to do next. If only the newspaper, sheet metal, and random pieces of wood on the lab floor were more comfortable.

Before I can even try lying down I hear a pounding on the door. "Kayla? You in there?" It's Kayla's mom, and she sounds mad. Mom always tells me to say angry not mad. Mad is for dogs and angry is for people, she says.

But right now, Kayla's mom sounds like a mad dog baying at us.

"Kayla Jeffers, come out right this instant! What are you kids playing at? Spud, are you in there?"

Great, even other people's parents call me Spud. There is no escape from potatoes.

"Mom, we're busy!" Kayla shouts back, giving no sign of getting up to open the shed door. To us she whispers, "Don't worry, she has a short attention span. If we ignore her she'll go away in a minute or two."

Doesn't sound that way to me.

"I can hear you, young lady!" she shouts from outside the door. "And believe me, later on we're going to have a nice long talk about respect. But right now I have to know what you're doing kidnapping Spud McKinley from his home, huh?"

Kidnapping? Kayla mouths to me. Then out loud shouts back, "I don't know what you're talking about, Mom. We just came over here to play."

"Plort play?" he asks.

"What was that?" Mrs. Jeffers asks sharply. "Who else do you have in there besides Spud and Felipe? Open the door!"

"It's just us," Kayla assures her, silently shushing Plort. "That was, er, Spud's phone playing a YouTube video."

"Well, if Mr. Spud has his phone out he should be well aware that his mother has been trying to reach him for the last hour. I've had to get a huge earful myself, so now it's your turn. Spud, call your mama back. And Kayla, get your hindquarters out here right now!"

"You can't open the door!" I whisper, praying that Mrs. Jeffers's ears aren't as keen as I think they are. "She'll see Plort."

"Hide him!" she whispers back.

Felipe, looking cool as the other side of the pillow, puffs on his fingernails, polishes them on his shirt, and says, "Just leave this to me. Mothers are my specialty."

Then while I frantically shove Plort back into my backpack, he unlocks and opens the door, sliding out and closing it almost all the way behind him before Mrs. Jeffers can get more than a quick peek inside.

"Mrs. Jeffers, how nice you look this morning!" he gushes. "May I say, that's a lovely scarf you have on your hair. Brings out the green in your eyes."

Through the crack I can see her staring suspiciously at Felipe. "It's a kerchief, and it's to keep the sweat from dripping into my eyes, not a fashion statement. Will you kindly tell Kayla to get out here and watch her little brothers and send Spud on his merry way so I can relax for one minute before work without his mom calling me back?"

"You sure do work hard, Mrs. Jeffers," Felipe says soothingly. "And you deserve a break more than any mom I know." I can see that she's softening. Gosh, I have to admire his technique. I wonder if it would work on my mom. Nah, I bet it only works on mothers you aren't actually related to.

"You should try telling Kayla that," Mrs. Jeffers says. "Always hiding out here in the shed and avoiding work."

"Oh, she's not avoiding work. She's actually working really hard. Do you know that she's probably going to invent something that will save the planet someday?"

"Really?" Mrs. Jeffers says, sounding impressed. "Like something that will stop climate change?"

"Um, something like that. Or maybe something about space exploration. You know, new worlds to live on if we can't live on Earth anymore for *some reason*." Felipe casts a meaningful glance back through the door crack at me.

"I knew she was playing around with old electronics, but I never realized she was thinking about such important matters. So she really is working out here, not just goofing off?"

Felipe gives her his most ingratiating smile. "You know she gets her work ethic from you, right, Mrs. Jeffers? She sees how hard you work every day to take care of your family, all by yourself. Do you know, I heard someone in town say just the other day that they've never seen a better run Dollar Diva. If you're the manager, it must be because of you. Kayla really admires you."

Kayla rolls her eyes. Felipe might be telling the truth, even if Kayla wouldn't admit it—but he's laying it on a little thick. Still, Mrs. Jeffers seems to be eating it up. At least it is keeping her from investigating what's going on inside the shed.

"Well, I do work hard, and I'm glad she appreciates everything I do. But that doesn't get her out of watching her brothers while I'm at work. Kayla!" she bellows into the shed. "You have five minutes, not a second more!" She looks at her watch. "Shoot, I have to shower!"

Felipe saunters back in. "What did you think of the master at work? Told you I can charm moms."

Plort pokes his head out of the Adventure Bag. "Plort?" he asks.

"Yeah, we're okay for now. She left. Hey, Felipe, how about you go over to my house and see if you can sweet-talk my mom for me?" I take out the phone and grimace at the notifications. "Scratch that. Even your mom-charm can't get me out of this."

My phone is flashing like crazy. I'd left it on. But now that I turn off do-not-disturb, I see there are twenty-three missed phone calls.

I click on the voicemail notification and put it on speaker. "You have twenty-three new messages," the pleasant computer voice tells me. Mom left a new message for each call? That's serious. "First message," my phone announce.

Then all heck breaks loose.

"*Sampson Augustus McKinley where are you I insist you answer your phone at once what is the meaning of this you can't just run off without telling me I was calling you and you KNOW you heard me this slime what is this slime I wake up in the morning and first there's raccoons and then some kind of gunk all over the plants and it can't be a coincidence that you kids were out there was it one of your science experiments or some kind of . . .*"

BEEEEEEEP.

"Next message," the computerized voice says as happily and calmly as if there wasn't a furious mother chewing my ear off in an unpunctuated stream-of-consciousness rant without pause for a breath.

"*Sampson you answer your phone right now or I'll take it away from you for a year why do you think we got you a phone you'd better answer when I call I know you're there mister if you don't call me back right now and explain yourself you'll be grounded until you're forty-five and my grandchildren will have to go to school in an Uber because you STILL won't be allowed out of the house to drive them . . ."*

BEEEEEEEP.

It goes on like that, twenty more times, until the last message:

"Er, hi, Spud. I think you should come home. I'm really worried about the potatoes, and about you, too. Love you kiddo."

That's Dad. Somehow his message is the one that makes me jump up.

"I have to get home," I tell my friends and the alien. "You stay in the lab and . . ."

"You heard my mom," Kayla says. "I have to get inside and watch my little brothers."

"Okay, well, at least you can stay with Plort, right, Felipe? Maybe you two can . . ."

"Sorry, spud. My dad got us VIP tickets to the new exhibit at the planetarium, and I have to be home . . ." He looks at his watch. "Ten minutes ago."

"So who's going to stay with Plort?" I ask, frantic.

Kayla shrugs. "He can stay here, I guess. Thing One and Thing Two are probably too afraid to look in the shed, after all the centipedes I bring inside and throw at them."

Plort and I look at each other. I think of him crammed in that tiny spaceship, hurtling though the universe, all alone while that scary Tantrunium tries to shoot him out of the sky.

"Plort Spud," he says adamantly.

"Definitely Plort Spud," I tell him. "I won't leave you alone." I sigh. "Guess I'll smuggle you back in the Adventure Bag. But the spaceship has to stay here. Kayla, are you sure the twins won't get nosy?"

"I'll be keeping an eye on them," she says, then goes to the corner of the shed, where she pries up a corner of the layers of newspaper that cover the dirt. I see the earth below heave and squiggle. After careful deliberation she chooses an earwig from the assortment of creepy crawlies that unobtrusively share her lab. "And if they forget to be afraid of my lab, this ought to remind them!"

She goes into her house, and a minute later I hear Mrs. Jeffers's station wagon pull out of the driveway. I turn to Felipe. "Can't you tell your dad you can't go? That something more important came up?"

He looks like I just suggested he slap a teacher. "But . . . this is family time. At a planetarium!" He grins like of course I should understand his priorities. "I have to get going. Call me later?" he says and leaves the lab.

"Looks like it's just you and me now, Plort," I say once Felipe has left.

Plort waddles over to the open backpack. "Plort 'venture?"

"I think more 'venture than I bargained for," I say as he scrambles inside the Adventure Bag.

I talk to Plort as I pedal home. I can't hear his answers very well, but it feels good just to have someone to vent to. Anyone who sees me probably thinks I'm crazy and talking to myself.

"I can't believe they left us! Don't they realize how serious this is? There's an enemy coming for us!"

"Plort not Spud," he squeaks.

"Yeah, but I already told you, I'm your friend. That means if someone's your enemy, they're my enemy too. Or to put it in your way of talking—Spud *is* Plort."

I just wish my friends saw it that way, too. Don't they know what it means to be loyal?

Now I'm not a third wheel. I'm a unicycle.

I don't know if I can deal with this alone.

"And in just a little while I'll have to face my parents," I moan. "I'd definitely like some backup for that."

"Plort help? Plort go backward?"

"Backward? Oh, back up! I get it. No, Plort, you can't help. I can't let my parents see you. Thanks for offering, though. It's more than *some* people do." People who are supposedly my friends.

I swallow down the feelings of being overwhelmed by Plort's plight and the bitter taste of my friends abandoning me in my time of need, and pedal as hard as I can. Maybe if I get there fast I can shave just a tiny bit off mom's fury.

I doubt it, though.

When I pull into our long gravel driveway, there is Donnie Webster again. He's just on his side of the property, leaning against a tree, grinning from ear to ear. That big backpack is at his feet.

I don't like the look of that at all. If Donnie Webster is smiling, it can't be good news for me.

CHAPTER 12

MA POTPOT!

My parents and I have a pretty good relationship but it's changed since I hit double digits; they're always worrying about me, not trusting me to make good decisions. I'm not really what you call the rebellious type. I might grumble a little, but when they tell me to do something I usually do it. And I have to admit, they try to be understanding. Except when it comes to helping with Lord of the Fries.

"You know, Sampson," Mom told me once, "there are kids all over the world working a lot harder than you. Kids work in mines, factories . . . all kinds of dangerous things."

"Yeah, but I remember you and Dad donated

money last year to help kids forced to work in the diamond mines in Sierra Leone."

This stopped her for a minute. Then she said, "Well, but those kids get overworked and abused, and can't go to school. You, on the other hand, are just asked to do your fair share."

"Doesn't seem fair to me," I muttered.

"Excuse me?"

"Other kids just have to think about school and homework. That's their job. Then when they have free time they can focus on their social life. You're stunting my social development by making me work!"

Mom laughed and scrunched her fingers in my hair. "You're going to be a great lawyer someday, Spud. But for now, you're a potato peeler." She flicked me with the potato-drying towel.

I complain, but Mom and Dad cut me slack whenever they can. They know how important my friends are to me. Like last night, having the sleepover. Mom and Dad worked extra hard getting everything ready for the weekend fry rush so I could enjoy time with my friends. I might have had to cut the morning short, but at least I got a fun night with them. So it isn't all bad.

It just feels like it sometimes.

But in a weird way I'm proud of all the hard work I do. I consider Lord of the Fries just as much mine as it is theirs. It's a family business. What other eleven-year-old can say he runs a business? I like it when Dad goes through the books and ends the ledger in black ink instead of red. That means we made a profit! When I look at the house, the food truck, the land we own, I feel like I really contributed to all of it.

Which makes it *so much worse* today when I roll up the driveway and see the deeply disappointed looks on Mom and Dad's faces.

I think she got all of her yelling out of her system in those twenty-two messages, because now she's standing with her arms folded across her chest, glaring at me. Dad's standing beside her, looking a little confused.

He's actually the first one to speak. "Did you do it on purpose, Spud?" he asks quietly. Then he looks over to the potato fields. Our life, our livelihood, our future.

"What?" I squeak. "No, of course not!"

Mom seems to take this as an admission of guilt. "How could you do it, Sampson?"

"I didn't do it, I swear!"

"You know all about it, though, don't you? I thought maybe you'd deny it, say *what are you talking about, Mom*?" Mom shakes her head. "But you obviously know what happened. Why did you do it?"

"I DIDN'T DO ANYTHING!" I shout. How come they're the ones who sound calm, and I'm the one yelling?

"Look, Spud, we just need to know what it is," Dad says. "What did you and your friends get up to last night?"

"Was it one of Kayla's experiments?" Mom asks. "Her mom told me she once blew up part of the garage."

"It was the shed, and it wasn't really an explosion, just kind of a dramatic *pouff!*" I tell her. "But no, she wasn't doing any experiments."

"Was it one of those alien gel kits you always wanted when you were a kid?" Dad asks. "The ones we wouldn't get you because we said we could make it from ingredients we had at home, but then we never did? Was it our fault? Did we let you down?"

Tears start to well in my eyes and I blink them away before they get any worse. "You've never let me down," I say, and mean it.

But I'm seriously tempted to answer yes to his first question. That would be the easy way out. At museum gift shops and toy stores they always had those make-your-own-goo kits. Dad's right, no matter how much I whined I never got one. How simple it would be to say that as soon as I was left alone I got out the borax, glue, and food coloring and went to work.

Lying would cover for the presence of Plort and his ship.

It would also make me look like an insensitive jerk who didn't care about his family.

And of course, they'd find out it wasn't regular joke slime once they looked a little closer. Especially once the apparently living, thinking slime looked at *them* in return! It won't take much observation for them to realize this is no ordinary goo.

"Dad, Mom, I can tell you honestly that I have no earthly idea what that slime is."

Strictly speaking, that's a true statement.

I go on, hurrying to explain, "When I saw it last night I figured it was just some kind of . . ."

"You saw it *last night*?" Mom interrupts sharply. "What time last night?"

"Er . . ."

"Why didn't you wake us up, Spud?"

"It was the middle of the night. You're always saying how tired you are. Bone-tired, Mom. That's what you say."

"But something like this?" Mom says, her voice rising. Maybe she didn't quite get all her yelling out of her system with her twenty-two messages. "Some kind of contamination on the potatoes? You'd wake us up if there was a fire, wouldn't you? Or a tornado? Something that could kill us? Well, this slime, whatever it is, could kill our business!"

I'm really sorry, I truly am, but I feel myself getting angry, too. I didn't ask for this to happen. I'm just as confused and upset about it as they are. But I knew it. I knew they would blame me for another thing that I didn't do.

"It's not my fault!" I rage back at them. "I didn't do anything wrong. I was out there, trying to forget about work, happy not to be stuck with stupid potatoes and stupid grease, serving stupid fries to stupid customers! I just wanted to have one last good time with my friends!"

Mom presses her lips together. Dad looks quietly disappointed.

"I'm surprised at you, Spud, I really am," Dad says while I stand huffing in the yard in front of them.

"Whatever happened, I expected you to step up and take responsibility for your mistakes," Mom adds. "That's the way we raised you."

"But Mom!"

She shakes her head slowly at me. "I thought you were better than that, Sampson. Turns out you're just a typical tween. No common sense, no consideration for anyone around you. Just an irresponsible, dramatic tween."

I look at them, mouth open, the hurt oozing from my skin as if it were the slime in the field. How can they think that of me?

Well, maybe because I haven't told them the entire truth.

But still!

"We have a lot of work to do today, Sampson," Mom says wearily. "Not only do we have to get everything ready for the food truck today, but now before we go we have to try to wash that slime off the crops. And just hope that it hasn't caused any damage."

"And we'd better do it before the sun gets any

higher," Dad adds. "The heat might bake whatever that is on."

"You'd just better hope it does wash off, mister," Mom says, shaking her finger at me.

Dejected, I start to head past them to the house. I'll take Plort to my room, maybe take a nap, and try to figure out what to do next.

"Where do you think you're going?" Mom asks, blocking my path. "While we're doing all that, you have to take care of Tooba. It's time for her hydroponic liquid medium to be changed, and you need to update her sunlight settings to Autumn mode. And don't forget to rotate her."

"And Spud?" Dad adds. "Take this seriously. Tooba is the most important thing to us."

"More important than me?" I ask in a small voice.

"Don't be silly, you know what he means," Mom says.

But right now, I'm not sure. Plus, she didn't actually answer my question, so who knows. If an alien came down and tried to kidnap me and Tooba, I'm not certain which one of us they'd try to save first.

With Plort still on my back, hidden in the Adventure Bag, I shamble over to the barn. As I go, I look at the fields again. The slime hasn't spread beyond where it was earlier, thank goodness. It has surrounded the barn, but stopped in its tracks at the concrete foundation that extends beyond the barn walls.

What's going to happen to us if the rest of the crop is lost? The potatoes out there represent another six months' worth of fries. Our income for the whole winter is underground. We thought it was safe, tucked in like little potato babies in a cozy bed of earth, sleeping until they're big enough to eat. (Okay, that sounds kind of weird, but just forget about eating babies and think about what I actually mean.)

We planned for the regular things that can hit a farming family. Gophers? Check! Potato beetles? The praying mantises we hatched took care of them. Fungus? Mom has this trick with baking soda.

When we first started growing potatoes we made a lot of mistakes. We were so anxious that we harvested them too small. We worried they might be drying out, so we overwatered them. Mom played opera to them.

Yeah, you heard that right. There have been lots of experiments showing that plants grow better if you play them music. And it's completely true. Mom figured plants would like something classical and sophisticated, but when she put the speakers in the fields the potatoes hardly grew at all.

Turns out potatoes like speed metal and noisecore.

Our neighbors? Not so much. For once Mom had to pay attention to the Websters' complaints, and the music experiment was finished. Now the potatoes just have to make do with Mom and Dad's loving and scientific care. They seem to be thriving.

Or . . . they were.

It's okay, I tell myself as I look at the slime. All's not lost. Sure, we'll lose out an entire season of income. We'll be late on a few bills. Might have to refinance the mortgage. I don't know what that means, exactly, but sometimes when I overhear Dad talking about the accounts he brings this up as a possibility. Mom always flatly refuses, just like she refuses to put any of our bills on a credit card. "Those Websters got their shiny truck and fancy TV ads on credit. Do you know how much they owe to the bank? We're not going to do that. If we can't afford it, we don't buy it—plain and simple."

But what if we can't afford a roof over our heads?

I feel so terrible. I mean, it's not my fault, exactly. But why do I feel like it is?

I wish that whole conversation had gone differently. If they'd just calmly asked me what happened instead of being all sad and mad and stuff, then I wouldn't have started yelling. Then I might have told them what really happened. They're good people, kind and understanding—about anything that doesn't affect their potatoes, anyway. Maybe if things had been different we'd all be sitting around the kitchen table—Plort included—brainstorming about how to save the potatoes and get Plort his ma potpot.

Well, I think as I unfasten the lock, *at least we have Tooba.*

With Tooba, we can always start over. I won't let anything happen to Tooba.

I take off my shoes so I don't track any slime inside, and open the barn door.

The barn is bright now, simulating daylight. There is Tooba in all her tuberous glory, basking happily in her fake sun. No clouds mar her sunbathing. No storms disturb her. Her life is peaceful, perfect, and protected.

"Hi, Tooba," I say, opening the Plexiglas dome that shelters her from the outside world. I give her a little pat. "How are you doing today?"

Tooba doesn't answer. She never does. She's the strong, silent type.

I unsling the Adventure Bag and set it down in front of our most prized possession. "Hey, Plort, there's someone I want you to meet." I unzip the bag. "Well, maybe not exactly some*one*, but . . ."

Plort stares at it in shock. His purple eyes get so enormous I thing they're going to pop out of his head.

He jumps out of the bag.

He grins at me.

He points at Tooba.

"MA POTPOT!"

CHAPTER 13

TOOBA'S SECRET

Plort is capering like a baby goat in springtime. He's so excited that he starts bouncing just like he did when we escaped from the cellar. He's pointing at Tooba and laughing like a maniac, saying over and over again, "Ma potpot! Ma potpot!"

I cradle my head in my hands, shaking it back and forth. He can't mean what I think he means.

Our Tooba can*not* be his ma potpot.

"Spudspudspud!" he says, bouncing over to me. "Plort saved. Everyplort saved!"

I try to smile back, but I'm not very convincing.

"Spud know? Spud surprise? Good Spud! Funny Spud!" He makes that gurgling squeak that is his version of a laugh.

He thinks I knew. He thinks I set this up as a wonderful surprise to give him exactly what he was looking for. To save the day.

If it had been anything else in the world, I would have helped him get his ma potpot. But Tooba is literally the one thing I can't give him.

There has to be some kind of mistake. How can a giant, perfectly tasty potato be a weapon?

"Plort, calm down a minute and listen to me. This isn't a ma potpot. You said it was a weapon. What are you going to do, throw this at Tantrunium's head?"

Plort chuckles again, still bouncing up and down a little bit. "Funny Spud!" I hate to break his heart. For the first time since he rolled out of the spaceship he doesn't look worried or scared. He actually looks happy. He's bouncing, making jokes . . . and I have to crush all that.

I have to disappoint him, just like I disappointed my parents.

I wish Kayla and Felipe were here. Somehow, hard things don't feel quite so hard when your friends are nearby. But they're off gallivanting on their own adventures. They don't care enough to help me *or* Plort.

"Plort, sit down a minute and listen, okay?" He

bounces over to me, having no idea I'm about to smash his hopes and happiness. "The thing you call ma potpot we call Tooba—and it belongs to us. Our whole business depends on Tooba. It isn't a weapon—it's food. Delicious food that humans love to eat. They give us money for it."

Plort cocks his round body to one side. "Moh . . . neeee?"

"Um, money, you know, they give rectangular pieces of paper, in exchange for fries."

"Pay-per? Ah, treeparts. Treeparts is moh-nee? Why treeparts?"

Treeparts? Oh, paper is made from trees, so that's probably as close as his broken translator can get. "The treeparts aren't actually worth anything themselves. We just all agree that they are. And then we trade them for things we need." Put that way, money doesn't make all that much sense.

"Of course, most of the time they pay with plastic," I add, which makes everything even muddier.

"Perpetual polymers?" Plort asks.

"Never mind," I groan. "The point is that ma potpot—I mean Tooba—is ours. I'm sorry, Plort, but you can't have her."

His lower lip starts to tremble. "MA POTPOT IS EVERYPLORT'S!" he shouts. "NEED MA POTPOT OR TANTRUNIUM SPLAT!" He claps his hands violently together. He says a few other things, but now he's talking so fast that the translator is overwhelmed and starts to smoke. He stomps around with a maniacal grin on his face, then he hunkers down looking scared. He's miming something, but I can't tell what.

"Look, Plort, what makes you even think that this is yours? This is from Earth. It's a potato. There have been potatoes on Earth practically since there *was* an earth. It's a very special, delicious potato, but just a potato."

Then I have a bright idea. "If you need potatoes, we have plenty of them. Or better still," I add, since I still don't want Plort to take our crop of first generation potatoes made from Tooba, "why not go to Super Mart and buy all the potatoes you need?"

He points again to Tooba. "Not Earthling—Plortling! Ma potpot from Plort." He stamps his little foot.

"No, Plort, you're wrong. Tooba came from . . ."

Then I stop cold, my spine tingling. I remember the night that Mom found Tooba about a year after we moved to Solanum.

It was summer. We'd already tried a few other crops and were having some success, but not much. Mom was thinking about switching to something new—herbs, maybe. Oprah had said rosemary was the next big thing.

We went out one evening just after sunset to watch the last of the fireflies. They'd been swarming the yard for a few weeks, but that night there are only a few stragglers left in the tall unmown grass.

This was before I'd met Felipe and Kayla. I hadn't made any real friends here yet, and I was still kind of upset about leaving Manhattan. But that night, with those fireflies, I thought for the first time that the country might be a really special place. I first started to glimpse the wonder of life in a wild place, free of skyscrapers and smog.

Then Mom said, "Look up!"

I did, and it looked like there were fireflies in space, too. Shooting stars! Every few seconds I'd see one zooming across the sky. "Make a wish!" Mom told me. "There! There's another! And another!"

I must have made a thousand wishes that night. I don't remember most of them. What does a second grader wish for? Unlimited candy, no bedtime. Maybe an electric scooter.

I only remember one of my wishes. I wished for friends.

Then, while I was alternating between the light show in the lawn and the light show in the stars, we saw a flash light up the sky.

"Heat lightning?" Mom wondered. "If a storm's coming, let's go in." She stood up and went inside.

"Coming," I said, but I lingered to get a last look at the sparkling, dancing, zooming lights. Just then I saw another meteor, bigger than any of the others. The other shooting stars had been like thin silver pencil lines drawn across the sky. This one was fat like a Sharpie line, with a big golden orb at the head.

"Mom, come back! There's a huge one!" I ran inside to get her, but then we heard a boom and she closed the door.

"What did I say? A summer storm. Well, there should be more fireflies tomorrow. Head upstairs and get ready for bed."

The next morning Mom found a giant potato in the middle of the onion field we'd just planted. "That's strange," she said. "Maybe it got in among the seed onions and fell out of the wheelbarrow yesterday. But I never noticed it."

It was the biggest potato we'd ever seen, and it gave Mom an idea. She started experimenting with the giant tuber—which she named, appropriately, Tooba—and finally produced the first generation potatoes we know and love.

I never connected those events—the flash, the boom, finding Tooba. Now that I think about it, it is a lot like what happened last night. Flash! Boom! And then . . . something alien in the field.

Tooba is an alien potato?!

A heavy feeling of dread settles in the pit of my stomach. Whichever way this goes, someone is going to be devastated. Either my family, because we lose our livelihood. Or Plort, because he loses the thing that can help him.

I still don't really understand why he needs Tooba, though. I get that there's an enemy, this Tantrunium. From Plort's pantomimes he seems to be a pretty scary dude. But how dangerous is he, really? Is he like a mean landlord who wants Plort to move?

Or is he more like a savage warlord who wants to erase Plort and his people from the galaxy?

I have a terrible feeling I know which one Tantrunium is.

What I still don't get, though, is how a potato can help. Even a superlative space potato.

"Plort, I know it's hard for us to communicate, but I need you to tell me more about how Tooba—I mean ma potpot—can help you."

Plort starts talking a mile a minute again.

"No, you have to slow down. The translator can't keep up."

He thinks for a moment, then starts talking again, very slowly. "Ma potpot super potpot. Big potpot." He shakes his rotund little body in frustration. "Plort big. Everyplort big. Aaarghh!" He flaps his little mitten hands, extremely agitated. I know he has something really important to explain but the translator just won't work right.

"It's okay, Plort. Take a deep breath and try again."

"Tantrunium strong," he says. He stands up on his tiptoes and stretches his arms as high as they'll go. Even though they don't actually reach higher than his head I get the general idea.

"Plort small." He hunkers down. "Everyplort small. Tantrunium smush squash squish!"

Okay, that I understand.

"But how does Tooba help?"

"Ma potpot make Plort . . ." He raises his arms again, puffs out his cheeks, and stomps across the room.

"Uh, I don't get it. Sorry Plort."

Plort makes a strangled sound of frustration. "Plort show!" he says, and heads for the Adventure Bag. With his back to me he rummages through it and finally takes something out. But I can't see what it is yet.

Then suddenly he turns and makes a run for Tooba. I can see what he has now—the multi-tool.

He's unfolded the knife blade and he's lunging right for Tooba!

Without even thinking about my own safety I try to tackle him, but he bounces out of my grasp and I slide on the floor, sprawled out. Plort springs up onto the hydroponic chamber where innocent, helpless Tooba is resting.

"Ma potpot!" he shouts triumphantly with the knife raised.

He's going to murder Mom's potato!

"Noooooo!" I cry.

But he doesn't stab Tooba. Instead he clings onto

the hydroponic chamber and, with the precision of a surgeon and a loving look in his eyes, slices off the teeniest, tiniest piece of alien space potato.

Then, as I watch incredulously, he hops down, opens the barn door, and dips the slice of Tooba in the slime that surrounds us.

Back inside with the door closed, he stands facing me.

"Spud watch," he says, and takes a nibble of the slime-covered raw potato.

For a second Plort is his normal small gummy-bear self. Then I blink . . .

And when I open my eyes, Plort is a giant.

Well, he's just a little taller than me, but for Plort he's a giant!

His body is different too. Before, he was soft and round and squishy. Now that squish has reformed into hard, sleek, buff *muscles*!

His smile is just the same, though—a two-toothed, gummy grin.

"See?" he says. "Plort embiggens!"

He strolls over to where I'm still sprawled on the floor. I don't think my legs will work. I'm in utter shock. Then he reaches down and scoops me up under the armpits. Without any effort at all he picks me up high over his head. "Plort powerful!" he says, laughing. "Tantrunium nothing!"

He sets me down, and I stagger a moment before finding my balance.

"Spud punch!"

"No, I can't . . ."

"Punch!"

So I give him a make-believe punch to the stomach. My knuckles bounce off some invisible wall. I grin and punch him harder. The only thing that happens is that my fist hurts. I can't touch him. There's some kind of force field around his body. But I could touch him when he picked me up, so I guess the barrier somehow senses violence and just stops that.

"I can't believe it! It's like spinach—and you're Popeye!"

"No, eye don't pop out," he says. "Muscles do!"

"No, I meant . . . never mind. This is amazing. Would it work for me, do you think?" How cool would that be to suddenly be five times my usual size.

Before he can argue I snatch the remaining saucy

sliver of Tooba out of his hand and take a bite. Only once it's in my mouth do I wonder if it will hurt turning into a giant. I remember getting growing pains when I had a growth spurt. That was bad enough, and the growth took place over a year. What will happen if my bones stretch five feet all in a second?

But when I chew, nothing happens.

Except . . .

My mouth thinks it's died and gone to heaven.

Now, as delicious as potatoes are in most forms, they're usually pretty disgusting raw. But this bite, with that slime-sauce on it . . . wowsers! It's like someone invented a whole new flavor of complete deliciousness! Kind of salty, kind of savory, but with an undertone of . . . amazing? I don't even have the words for it.

I lick a tiny bit of the goo by itself, and get a rush of taste sensations that leaves my tongue dizzy. My mouth starts watering, and the only thing I want in the world is more of this sauce.

I take one more small bite of the two together, Tooba and goo, and somehow it's even better than the delectable sauce alone. It's like the two were made for each other.

And this is on a raw potato. Just imagine it on delicious fries!

"That's out of this world!" I tell Plort.

He chuckles. "But no bigspud."

"I don't care if it doesn't make me a giant," I tell him. It sounds cool but it would probably get annoying really fast—bumping my head on door frames, not being able to fit in my bed.

"Plort, you don't understand," I go on after I finish the last bite. "No one on Earth has ever tasted anything like this. This is amazing. Do you know what people would pay?"

Plort shakes his head.

"Neither do I, but I tell you, this would be a sensation! Tooba and slime! Who would have guessed?"

This combination could save Lord of the Fries! The slacking business would completely revive. People who had been lured over to Fry King would return in droves.

Plort is looking at me funny, and I realize what I'm saying, and what I'm thinking.

"Tantrunium smush everyplort," Plort says. "But bigplorts protect!"

I don't understand every detail of Plort's problem,

but it is crystal clear that Plort and his people are in danger. And thanks to his demonstration, I now realize exactly how Tooba can help him. A planet full of giant, muscular, invincible Plorts could stop any enemy.

I also realize how much Tooba and the slime can help my family.

But I promised I'd help him. He's my friend. He trusts me.

Losing Tooba will kill my family's business.

Not having ma potpot might very well literally kill Plort and the others of his kind.

It's really not much of a choice, it is? Of course I have to give Tooba to Plort.

But there has to be another way! Some way that both of our families could be saved . . .

Then there's a jarring knock on the door, and we both jump. The door swings slowly open. "Spud, are you in there?" my dad calls. "I have to show you something. You're not going to believe this!"

Really, at this point I'm ready to believe almost anything.

I dash over and slip out the door before he can open it enough to see the giant Plort, and close the door behind me.

"Spud, life is looking up again!" Dad says, his eyes dancing with delight. "You know that slime all over the potatoes? Well, I tasted it, and . . . Just wait until you try it. This is going to be a game changer for Lord of the Fries."

He's so happy, so enthusiastic, talking about new advertising and social media campaigns and other ways to get the word out about this wonderful new fry sauce.

"This is going to save us, Spud!"

Yeah, but it's going to doom Plort.

CHAPTER 14

SPECIAL SPUD SAUCE

"I'll be right there, Dad," I tell him. "I just have to finish up with Tooba."

"Okay, Spud, but don't take too long. You can always change Tooba's hydroponic fluid tonight. We have to get all this slime harvested right away so we can have it ready when the first customers arrive. Which they will . . ." He checks his watch. "Within the hour! Hurry!"

He runs back toward the field with a bucket and shovel.

Back inside the barn, Plort is already starting to shrink. Now he's exactly my size, and his muscles are starting to look a little flabby.

"Plort, I need you to stay here with ma potpot," I

tell him. “And listen: I promised I would help you, and I will. You can trust me. But I have to trust you too. I know how much you need ma potpot, but my family does too. We have to think of a way that we can both get what we need.” I pull at my hair. Sleepless and stressed are not the ways I do my best thinking.

“After I finish up selling fries today, we’ll come up with something, together. I know we will! So promise me you’ll just stay put, you and Tooba, until I can come back for you. Okay?”

“Plort,” he says.

That’s funny, most of the things he says have been actual words lately. Weirdly arranged ungrammatical words, but still words. He hasn’t said a simple *plort* in a while.

Well, I guess that will do as a promise.

Outside, Mom and Dad are happier than I’ve seen them in a long time.

“Sampson, I’m sorry I got so mad at you,” Mom says, hugging me tight. “I don’t care what you kids got up to if the result is this delicious mess. How did you do it?”

“Er, I don’t know. It just kind of happened.”

"It wasn't an experiment? You don't know the ingredients?"

"No, we just woke up and it was kinda . . . there." That's mostly true.

"Well, never mind," she says cheerfully. "I have a friend at the university food science lab that can analyze just about any food compound. If he tests the slime he can break down its component parts and then maybe we can figure out how to synthesize it."

"Or it might just be part of the soil," Dad guesses. "A new kind of slime mold that evolved specifically in this location and only lives on potatoes."

"Only our special Tooba potatoes," Mom clarifies. "Oh, Sampson, this is the best day of my life! A new beginning for Lord of the Fries!" She's practically dancing.

Collecting the slime isn't very easy. In some places we just scoop it up with a shovel, mulch and all, and let it drain through cheesecloth to filter out all the bits of dirt and wood.

"Er, guys, this isn't exactly sanitary, is it?" I ask as I shovel another bunch of slime and dirt into a filter.

"Oh, nonsense," Dad says. "People should eat more dirt. It's good for the gut."

“Besides,” Mom adds, “since this is an organic farm, people don’t have to worry about eating anything we produce—even the dirt. No poisons and pesticides.”

I feel like the county health inspector might see things differently. But Mom and Dad are so enamored of this new sauce that they aren’t thinking clearly.

I have some other worries, too. The slime and potato combination had a dramatic effect on Plort, but it didn’t seem to do anything to me . . . yet. But what if there’s a delayed reaction in humans? What if in a few hours I turn into a twenty-foot-tall giant with the muscles of a world-class mixed martial arts fighter?

What if Mom and Dad do, too?

What about all the townies and tourists who are just about to eat our fry-and-slime combination? What if all of Solanum mutates into monsters? Or worse! It might do something completely different to humans. Maybe we’ll turn into reptiles, or gravity won’t affect us and we’ll go hurtling into the atmosphere! Anything could happen!

Gee, now I sound like Felipe. I really wish he and Kayla were here right now.

After we've scooped up a lot from the ground, we start scraping the slime off the plants themselves. This proves to be a much harder task. It's like it wants to stay on the potato plants. I'm using a squeegee on the leaves, and every time I scrape some into a cup it stretches as far as it can, trying desperately to hold on to the potato plant.

Pretty soon we've collected several bucket loads.

"There, that should be enough for now. Let's rev up the engine and heat up the oil, guys! It's time to roll out Lord of the Fries!"

When there are fairs or farmers markets we sometimes drive the old converted camper into town, but most of the time we just park it on the edge of our property and set up shop along the road, like kids with a lemonade stand. Since the food bloggers started talking about us it has been a surprisingly successful method. There's even a bus service from town to bring tourists out.

The only problem is that the Webster farm is closer to town than us. People see that shiny red truck with its stupid golden crown long before they see our humble food truck. Most of the time Rodney Webster is out in front in his ridiculous Fry King costume, waving his giant French fry scepter at passing cars.

Of course they stop there first. They came for fries, he has fries, and they never bother to look at the name. Locals know to go down the road a bit until they find us, but most of the tourists hit Fry King, come down to our farm to do a U-turn, and realize they made a mistake. Sometimes they'll buy another small bag of fries from us, but Fry King serves such massive amounts of his inferior fries that they don't have much appetite, even for our superlative fries.

Now, with a billion things on my mind, I start heating up the oil. I'm way behind on my peeling and slicing, so I'll have to do that as I go along. It's going to be a busy day, all of it stuck in the back of this cramped, sweltering food truck, dodging hot oil.

I realize suddenly that it has been hours since I worried about middle school. Well, that's something at least.

It's almost time. The first cars will be here any minute, when Mom shouts out, "What are we going to call it?"

"Huh?" Dad asks as he adjusts the sandwich board out front.

"The slime! We can't call it slime. I mean, it's already a weird color. No one eats greenish-blue goo. Once they take the first bite it won't be a problem—they won't want to stop. But we have to convince them to take that first bite. And for that we need a good name. We can't sell it as Fries with Random Green-Blue Goo from the Garden."

Actually, that's kind of catchy.

"How about Special Spud Sauce?" I suggest.

Mom likes the idea, but Dad makes it even better. "How about Spud's Special Spud Sauce? After all, this is because of you. Somehow." He scrunches up his face. "Exactly how did this slime spread?" Luckily, the first cars are pulling up, and Dad has to get to work. "Remind me to get to the bottom of this when we've finished with the lunch rush."

But the lunch rush never ends. As people taste the fry-and-sauce combo they start to rave about it. Word spreads online, and soon everyone knows to bypass Fry King and head straight to Lord of the Fries. The lunch crowd merges into the dinner crowd. Bus after bus makes the round trip from town to our farm. There's a line down the road half a mile long—all the way from us to Fry King.

But no one even looks at his gaudy truck. The only money the Websters make all day is from selling cold water to the sweaty people at the end of the line for Lord of the Fries.

We have the single most successful day in the history of Lord of the Fries. We never stop selling for a second. I have blisters on my fingers from paring and peeling bucket after bucket of potatoes. There are burns on my forearms from splashing grease.

But it is worth it, just to see those huge happy grins on Mom and Dad's faces.

If only it didn't have to end. There has to be a way to both help Plort and keep Tooba here! Unfortunately, I can't think what it could possibly be.

It's late afternoon when I hear a commotion from the line of people out front. "Hey, wait your turn," someone snaps. "Not fair!" a little girl whines.

I look out and see none other than Rodney Webster shoving his way to the front of the line.

"Stand aside, folks, I'm here on official fry business," he sneers, shoving and stepping on toes. When he's at the front he puts his elbows on the counter and says, "What have we here? You giving away free cash or something? These people can't be here for your fries. Who would want to eat out of this dirty, roach-infested truck?"

He looks over his shoulder and waggles his eyebrows at his son Donnie, who has stomped up behind him. He's still wearing that oversized backpack and if anything, it looks even more stuffed now.

Donnie gives a laugh that sounds like a donkey's bray. And you know what another word for donkey is, right?

"Looks like these people know something you don't, Rodney," Dad tells him. "Like what good French fries taste like."

"Now if you'll excuse us, we're trying to feed these nice people," Mom adds, glowering down at him.

Rodney doesn't seem at all disturbed. "How about you give me a sample. A free sample."

Dad is in the process of handing the next customer their fries when Rodney intercepts them.

"Hey!" the customer says.

"Don't worry," Dad assures them. "I'll make you another batch, extra large, extra hot."

"And extra Spud's Special Spud Sauce!" the customer demands. "That stuff was so good I got back in line for seconds." He turns to the person behind him. "I've been waiting in line since lunch, but I don't care. I *had* to have some more!"

Rodney and Donnie are standing off to the side, sharing their fries.

"What's this disgusting-looking stuff growing on them?" Donnie asks, sticking a finger in the green-blue sauce. "Ew, are you serving moldy fries?"

But then he takes a bite, and even he can't suppress a look of delight. It quickly passes, and he looks furious. So does his dad.

"What are you putting in here, McKinley?" he demands to know. "It can't be legal!"

Mom sticks her head out. "Speaking of legal, if you don't stop harassing our customers I'm going to call the police. Go back to your Fry King, Rodney."

He does, but he leaves with a wicked laugh. "Enjoy today, McKinley," he tells my dad then leans in to whisper, "Because I'm going to destroy you."

Donnie follows his dad, giving us an evil grin. As he leaves, I swear I see his backpack wiggle.

I'm immediately distracted as another busload of people pulls up. My entire life becomes a never-ending parade of potatoes, and I can't think of anything beyond peeling, paring, slicing, and frying.

Finally, near nightfall, when the crowd becomes more sparse, Mom and Dad say I can take a break. I run inside to the house to the bathroom (priorities!) and then immediately back to the barn to check on Plort.

He's not there.

Neither is Tooba!

CHAPTER 15

HAVE YOU SEEN THIS PLORT?

I stare at the empty hydroponic chamber. The liquid bubbles slowly; the tubes and wires hang limp and disconnected.

"Tooba?" I whisper in shock. "Plort?"

No, no, no . . . this can't be happening.

He promised! He promised he'd stay in the barn with Tooba until I was finished selling fries, and then we'd figure this out. If he'd just given me time we could have come up with a plan that would have helped us both.

I can't believe this. I search every corner of the barn, even shining my flashlight in the rafters overhead. Maybe he heard a noise and got scared so he hid somewhere.

But there's not a sign of him. Or Tooba.

How could he do this to me? I trusted him. And I thought he trusted me. I know I talked about how important his ma potpot is to my family, but did he really think I was going to put him and his people in jeopardy? That I was just going to selfishly keep Tooba for myself?

I thought he understood me better than that.

I guess he didn't know me at all. And I certainly didn't know *him* like I thought I did. I thought we were friends—a team! Now he's betrayed me. There's not even a chance that we can find a way to help both of our families.

What am I going to tell Mom and Dad?

And then, after a few minutes of pacing and hair pulling, I calm down enough to be able to think a little more clearly. Something isn't sitting right about all this. Then it hits me.

Why was Donnie carrying that big backpack? That big, overstuffed, *wiggling* backpack?

If I hadn't carried an alien in a backpack myself I'd never have guessed, but now that I think about it I have a terrible feeling that Plort was in Donnie's bag.

But it was more full than that. I think Tooba was in there too!

Donnie and the horrible Websters stole Tooba and kidnapped Plort.

But wait, I think as I continue to pace. Plort was perfectly capable of opening my backpack's zipper from the inside. If he wanted to escape from Donnie's bag he would have been able to any time he wanted.

That means that Plort wasn't kidnapped. He's working with the Websters! Plort must have tricked me, pretended to be my friend all this time, just so I'd bring him to Tooba.

Just so he can steal the one thing my family depends upon.

What if the story about Tantrunium is a complete fake, too? I think back to Plort's wide-eyed, innocent face, his fear, the dramatic way he pantomimed some kind of attack on his people. He seemed so genuinely frightened and desperate. Was it an act?

I feel so stupid. He used me to get what he wanted.

Felipe was right. Plort probably wants the ma potpot and slime combination superpowers so that he can take over the universe. And he probably made a deal with the Websters to give them all the special potatoes and secret slime they want. Now evil Plort will rule the universe . . . and the Fry King will rule the French fry business.

I have to get Tooba back from the Websters. But I can't do it alone. I reach for my phone, which I'm sure I left in the Adventure Bag, but it's not there. So I go inside and place frantic calls to Kayla and Felipe on the home phone. I don't know if they'll help but I don't have anyone else to ask.

It takes a lot of wheedling with their parents—after all, they just had a sleepover last night—but finally after a lot of calls back and forth they get permission to come for another sleepover tonight. My parents agree, too.

"We worked you so hard, you deserve some time with your friends," Dad says. "Good job today, Spud. I'm proud of you."

"How's Tooba?" Mom asks. "Did you change her growth medium and adjust the light settings?"

"Oh, Tooba's out of sight!" I say enthusiastically, giving her two thumbs-up.

It's not a lie. In fact, Tooba might be so out of sight that we never see her again.

I didn't give Felipe and Kayla many details over

the phone about what's going on. When they come into my room they're joking about something or other and hardly say hello to me.

I can't help it. I've been under so much stress, so sad and angry and worried about so many things, that I react in a huff. "This isn't the time for jokes, so if that's how you're going to be you might as well go home now. The Dynamic Duo can go watch stupid alien movies while the Third Wheel deals with an actual alien on his own!"

I hold open the door and gesture for them to leave again. They just stare at me.

"Spud, what's gotten into you lately?" Felipe asks.

"Yeah," Kayla says. "You're all prickly. And what's this about a third wheel?"

I stand with my hands on my hips. "Well, that's how I feel all the time lately. Like it's you two—best friends, next-door neighbors, hanging out whenever you want and doing amazing things together. And then there's me. I'm the extra."

I'm angry, but to my embarrassment I feel tears in my eyes. I blink them back fast before anyone notices.

My friends are silent for a moment. Then Felipe

says, "What's wrong with being extra? I mean, an extra's always something good, right? Like when someone says *now with extra chocolate*. If you're getting extra it's because it's something really special."

"And what's that nonsense about third wheel?" Kayla asks.

"It's just a saying," I mutter. "It means someone who's not needed or wanted."

"Well, it's silly. A third wheel is a tricycle, and what's wrong with that?"

"Maybe it's a fifth wheel, then," I say, starting to feel a little foolish.

"Fifth wheel is another name for an RV that you pull behind a truck, and camping is super fun. So what's wrong with a fifth wheel?"

"I think no matter how many wheels you put on something you just make it better and better," Felipe says with a smile.

"Yeah, so what do you care which wheel you are, Spud? If you want, I'll be the third wheel. You can be wheel number one. Does that make you happy?"

I smile and I feel completely dumb.

"We're all friends," Felipe says. "Best friends. Sure, we have different experiences. We don't always share the same things. But we're all equally close. I like you just as much as I like Kayla."

"Ditto," Kayla says.

I look at them sheepishly. "I'm sorry, guys. I guess I was just worked up about starting middle school, and all that stuff your sister said about friendships falling apart. I had this vision that you guys would hate me as soon as school started. Each time you shared a joke or a memory I wasn't involved in it made me feel like I was losing you."

"You're not going to lose us, Spud," Felipe assures me.

"Not unless you start complaining about wheels again," Kayla adds, punching me in the arm. "Dummy."

I never thought being called a dummy could make me feel so happy.

Now that my friends are back I'm full of self-confidence. "We have to get Tooba back," I tell them after I explain everything that happened today. "She has to be somewhere in the Websters' house. If we can get inside and get past Donnie and that sneaky, lying Plort . . ."

"You know," Felipe says, "I don't think Plort would

betray you like that." He puts his hands up, knowing it's a complete backtrack from what he said earlier. "It's just a feeling I have, Spud. I don't think he'd do you dirty."

"No way," Kayla said. "He really likes you. He trusts you. You were the only one who could really understand him."

"It could have been all an act," I say.

"Maybe," Felipe says. "But I think there must be some other explanation."

"Yeah," Kayla adds with a meaningful glare, "you should learn to have more faith in your friends, Spud!"

"Okay, guys, don't rub it in!" I groan.

We have to fake our way acting normal through dinner. As soon as we can, we slip outside. "Just to stargaze," I tell Mom. We're not pitching a tent tonight. Felipe and Kayla's sleeping bags are on my bedroom floor.

As quietly as we can, we sneak past the barn, around the slime-covered potato fields, up to the boundary of the Webster property. It is surrounded with rusty barbed wire, plastered with signs saying NO TRESPASSING.

“We’re not exactly trespassing,” I say as I hold up a section of wire for my friends to crawl under. “We’re retrieving stolen property.”

We tiptoe our way to the house. Luckily the moon hasn’t risen yet, and it’s almost completely dark. The house is mostly dark, too, with just one light on in the ground floor. Quiet as cats, we pad up to the house and crouch outside the window.

Then, motioning the others to stay down, I slowly rise and peek in.

There’s Tooba, sitting right on the kitchen table!

Illuminated by one dim overhead light, she looks all dried out and lonely, kind of bruised like she’s been manhandled. She must have gotten knocked around in Donnie’s backpack. If he’s hurt her . . .

None of the Websters are in the room. But then in the corner I see a dark shadow moving. It’s lurching, looming . . . and moving closer and closer to Tooba.

Then it comes into the light, and it’s all I can do not to cry out.

IT’S ANOTHER ALIEN!

CHAPTER 16

AND THEN THERE WERE TWO!

Its body is sickly gray, daubed with yellow blotches. It's about the same size as Plort, maybe a little bigger. But it looks altogether scarier. Where Plort's jade-green jelly-like body looks wholesome and clean, like candy, this creature looks like a fat slug that grew arms and legs.

No, that's not fair to slugs. I think slugs are cute. This round alien looks like a giant jelly bean that's gone bad.

I duck back down and tell my friends. They take a quick peek, but I whisper to them, "We can't all look in at once. If that thing sees us, we're toast!" So we agree that I'll keep looking while they crouch below the window with their ears pressed to the wall, trying to hear what's going on inside.

With one eye just peering around the side of the window, I watch what's going on inside. Like a predator stalking prey, the alien approaches Tooba, its arms reaching to pick it up. I can't stand the thought of that thing touching our precious potato.

Just then, Rodney and Donnie burst into the kitchen. The alien's arms drop but it holds its ground. It might be small, but it doesn't look at all intimidated by the Websters, even though they are huge in comparison.

Rodney, towering over the new alien, has his fists balled up. "No way!" I hear him shout. He's standing close to the window so I can hear him clearly. "I kept my part of the bargain, but you haven't kept yours. Don't think for a second you're getting your hands on this potato until I get what I deserve."

I think most adults would be scared of Rodney bowing up on them like this. He looks like he's about to take a swing at the alien. Rodney's not very muscular, but he's a big guy. There would be a lot of weight behind his punch.

Donnie, standing behind his dad, looks like he's waiting to see who the winner is before he chooses sides.

"Oh, you'll get what you deserve, all right," says a slippery voice. It's coming from the alien. Unlike Plort, he's speaking perfect English. Then I notice that he's wearing one of those communication devices around his head. It looks in much better shape than Plort's, no dings or missing pieces.

"If you try to take it without paying, I'll show you how Earthlings settle their disputes," Rodney says.

"Calm down, human. The bargain was made. As long as the green criminal doesn't obtain the potpot, General Tantrunium is content to wait until he arrives to take possession of it. And believe me, when you meet him, you'll get exactly what you deserve."

Then they all move to the other side of the kitchen and sit down at the table to glare at each other. I can hear them still talking inside, but now they're too far away for me to make out the words.

Finally Rodney jumps up, heads to the back of the house, and comes back pushing a dolly. I have to stand on my tiptoes to see what it's carrying—a big, heavy, metal safe.

Rodney's talking loudly again and he looks mad. "Since neither of us trust each other, I'm going to lock up your precious potato." He scoops up Tooba and throws her into the safe. I flinch—he's going to bruise her! "When you've paid me, you can have her back."

The alien starts waving his arms at the sight of the safe. "Stop! I command you . . ."

But Rodney is too fast. He slams the door, twists the combination lock, and sits down again with a look of smug satisfaction. After that, they all just glower at each other.

I slide back down to the ground and whisper, "So that wasn't Plort in Donnie's backpack."

"Right," Felipe says. "It must have been that other alien."

"And Tooba too. I bet Donnie and that other alien broke into the barn while I was in Lord of the Fries."

"It sounds like that alien and the Websters know each other?" Kayla asks.

"More like the Websters are mercenaries," I say, "helping that alien get ma potpot for Tantrunium. He's going to pay them for their help. See, I told you those Websters are total jerks."

"What happened to Plort, then?" Kayla asks.

I close my eyes, a nauseated feeling creeping over me. I left Plort all alone, knowing that evil aliens were after him. And then when he disappeared, my first thought was that he'd betrayed me.

Now, suddenly, I'm sure that something terrible has happened to him. This slimy, yellow-spotted alien talks in such a cold, heartless voice—he could have done something awful to Plort. Plort could be tied up right now on the cold floor of the Websters' bathroom, held prisoner until Tantrunium gets here.

(*General* Tantrunium? That's what the spotted alien said. A general is in charge of an entire army! This just keeps getting worse and worse!)

Or what if . . .

I bite my lip; it's too terrible to think about.

What if that other alien killed Plort?

I never should have left him alone. I should have defied my parents. I should have . . .

I feel a nudge on my shoulder, and when I look down I almost jump out of my skin.

At first I think I'm looking at a walking pile of laundry. I see Bermuda shorts, a heavy thermal shirt, white socks and sandals—all in little kid's sizes. Then I see Plort's big purple eyes peeking up at me from under a broad-brimmed Panama hat, and I grab him in a big hug. It's all I can do not to scream his name.

"Oh, Plort," I whisper. "I've never been so happy to see anyone! I thought you were a goner!"

"Plort gone," he whispers back, making a zooming motion with his hands. "Plort in potpothouse, and Speets come."

"Speets?" I ask.

"Tantrunium soldier. Bad, bad Speets." He points toward the window. Oh, the new alien is called Speets.

"How did he get in?" I ask.

"Spud nolock."

Oh boy! I was in such a hurry to get to the food truck I forgot to lock the barn door.

"Plort scared. Plort bounce." He sheds a green tear. "Plort no save ma potpot. No save everyplort."

"It's okay, Plort. We found Tooba—I mean ma potpot—again. She's in the Websters' house. Unfortunately, that scary alien is there, too. And Rodney and Donnie are sitting right there, guarding it. There's no way we can get it tonight."

Plort sheds another tear. "Plort lose ma potpot . . . again."

Again, I want to ask? But communication is so hard that it's probably not the right time. Instead I suggest we head back to my room for the night. Once we're out of earshot I ask the next important questions:

"Where on earth did you go, and what's with the weird outfit?"

Plort hands me a piece of newspaper, torn with ragged edges. "Super Mart," he says proudly. The newspaper shows an advertisement for the produce section, displaying mounds and mounds of potpots. Er, potatoes.

"Plort think many potpots. Maybe ma potpot."

"No, sorry, Plort. Those are just regular potatoes."

"Plort try slime. No bigness."

Well, that's a relief. Imagine if he'd grown to giant proportions in the middle of Super Mart!

"How did you even get there?" I ask him.

"Bounce!" he says proudly. "And use Spudtech!" He holds out my phone, with the mapping app up and showing the way to Super Mart. I'd left it in the Adventure Bag in the barn.

"You bounced all the way?" Kayla asks. "That's impressive."

Plort shrugs at the compliment. "Earth gravity not much. Plort bigbounce."

Then, after a lot of gibberish and gestures, Plort

manages to tell us that he was so scared at seeing his enemy Speets that he decided he needed to do something drastic. The first step was to get himself a disguise. To, er, pass as a human.

He's so proud of his idea that I don't have the heart to tell him that in his weird, mismatched clothes—which still have the price tags on them—he looks even more alien than he does as his usual self. With no clothes, maybe he could pass as an exotic tropical frog escaped from the zoo. In clothes the only thing he looks like is an alien dressed like someone's long-lost Uncle Bernie.

"Okay, I understand how you got to the store," Felipe says. "But once you were there, how did you move around inside without anyone freaking out? Someone must have seen you."

"Small humanperson help," he says.

With another game of charades he acts out what happened. After a long time of guessing we finally piece it together. When Plort snuck into the Super Mart, he lucked out and emerged right in the toy section. When he saw a human coming he bounced into a storage bin full of big inflated balls and sucked his arms and legs in. Just when he thought he was safe, a little girl saw him and dragged him out.

"Mama! Want!" she said.

"No, sweetie," her mother said.

But the little girl *really* wanted that ball. While her mother shopped, she bounced Plort all around the store, through the produce aisle, where he took a potato and tested it with some slime he brought . . . and through the kids' clothes section. Whenever he passed something he wanted, he just popped out an arm and grabbed it.

At the checkout line the mother put her foot down, and a stockboy was sent to bring Plort back to the toy aisle. He was just going to take the clothes away when his phone beeped. "Lunch break!" he said, and dumped Plort, clothes and all, back into the ball bin.

At least, this is what the three of us all working together came up with. It's a pretty unlikely story, so we might have gotten some of it wrong.

"So actually, you stole the clothes," Kayla says with disapproval. "You could get in trouble for that."

"Plort nosteal. Plort pay."

"With what?" I ask, dreading the answer.

Plort grins at me. "Treeparts!" he says . . . and gives me a handful of leaves.

We all roll on the floor laughing. Maybe Plort is terrified. I am, too. Maybe my future and his both hang in the balance. But at least we are all together, and that's a wonderful feeling.

"Well, I guess there's only one thing left to do now," I say when we catch our breath.

Plort nods, punches his fist in the air, and says, "Save ma potpot!"

CHAPTER 17

HOW TO SAVE A TOOBA

"We can't just break in!" Kayla says.

"Why not?" I ask indignantly. "They stole from me first. They came onto our property, snuck into the barn, and burgled our space potato. There's nothing wrong with taking it back."

"Well, maybe nothing morally wrong," Felipe says. "But it's still illegal! What are you going to do if they call the police and we all end up in jail?"

My friends have a point. I'm not just worried about getting in trouble myself. If police come, they'll see Plort, and before you know it the National Guard will be here. So we have to come up with another solution.

We wrack our brains until we're sleepy. Then suddenly I say, "If we can't break in, then we just have to get one of the Websters to invite us in."

"Good one, Spud," Felipe says. "Like they're ever going to do that."

A slow smile spreads across my face. "They just might!"

• • •

The next morning I make a big show of heading to the bathroom five or six times, stomping down the hallway loudly enough for my parents to hear. I make horrible retching noises sure to wake them up. Each time I leave, I dab water on my forehead to look like sweat.

Finally, they stagger out of their bedroom, their eyes pre-coffee blurry, and ask if I'm okay.

"Sick!" is the only word I can manage to choke out before I dash back to the bathroom and slam the door behind me. I fake another disgusting sound.

If I have one piece of advice for anyone, young or old, it's this: When you're pretending to be sick, never try to fake a cold or a fever. For one thing, it's too easy to disprove with a thermometer. And then, there's only so far you can go in making fake snot. There are even some people who will make you go to work or school even with a nasty cold.

But no one wants to be anywhere near someone who is throwing up. All it takes is good sound effects behind a closed door and you're good to go. Between bouts just look weak and self-pitying, and they'll buy it.

"I hope it wasn't Spud's Special Spud Sauce," Mom muses as I make my way unsteadily back to bed.

"Nah," Dad says. "You and I were eating it all day, and we're perfectly fine."

"Don't you guys want to head home?" Mom asks Kayla and Felipe. "You don't want to catch it."

"It's probably just something he ate," Felipe says.

"Yeah," Kayla adds. "I told him not to eat that marshmallow after it fell in the dirt."

"Okay, but you kids will be on your own today. We'll be manning Lord of the Fries until sundown again today."

Perfect. Exactly how we planned it.

As soon as my parents are gone we scour the woodpile at the back of our farm. "Caught him!" I say, and shove something wriggling into a pillowcase.

All the other preparations were accomplished last night.

Now we watch and wait.

From behind a thick hedgerow between our properties we watch the Websters' front door. By midmorning Rodney has fired up the Fry King truck and headed out to the main road with Donnie. As far as we can tell, Mrs. Webster is the only one left in the house.

Well, there's Speets, too, but he's not exactly going to answer the door.

"Sticky!" Plort says beside us. "Itchy!"

"Don't scratch," I caution him as he hops up and down, looking extremely uncomfortable. "We'll just have to start all over again."

He grumbles but stands still with his arms out, letting the paint we smeared all over his body dry.

"Are you guys ready?" I ask Felipe and Kayla.

"All set!" Kayla confirms, putting her backpack on her shoulders, and salutes.

"How about you, Plort? Do you know what you have to do?"

He tries to give a salute, but his short arms won't reach his forehead. Instead he sort of salutes his chin. "Plort ready!"

I take a deep breath as I pick up the Adventure Bag. This is a pretty complicated plan, and it depends on a lot of things going exactly right. But we've talked about it and rehearsed it in our heads so much last night and this morning that I'm feeling pretty confident.

I touch Plort's skin with one finger. "You feel pretty dry." I look at my finger. No yellow paint, though my arms are covered in bits of glue, little scraps of paper, and a few splashes of light brown paint.

Kayla and Felipe set off toward the Websters' house. Plort puts on a kids' yellow rain slicker, pulls the hood over his face, and snaps all the buttons shut. At first glance he looks like a regular little kid.

I wait until they're all gone, then I reach into the pillowcase. "Sorry about this, Boopsnoot," I tell the chubby snake as he emerges. He is brightly colored, with alternating dark and light blotchy stripes on his back, and bright orange-red markings on his neck and sides. His nose turns up in an adorable point. "I know being inside isn't your favorite thing, but I promise I'll bring you a nice plump frog after I let you go."

I rub Boopsnoot under the chin and then creep

after Felipe and Kayla. Instead of following them to the front door, though, I sneak up to the window at the side of the house.

We decided not to break in and take anything from their house. But after long debate we decided it was okay to break in to put something *into* their house. I pry open one corner of the screen and Boopsnoot slithers inside, just as Kayla and Felipe ring the doorbell.

"Coming!" I hear Mrs. Webster say.

"Hi, Mrs. Webster," Felipe says in that voice he saves especially to charm mothers. "Sorry to bother you on such a pleasant Sunday morning, but Donnie sent us to help you out."

"Oh really?" she asks skeptically. I can see the flaw in our plan. Even his mother knows that Donnie probably isn't going to do anything nice like helping his mother.

"Yes, ma'am. He saw it on the way out the door, but since his dad needed him to help with Fry King right away he didn't have time to catch it."

"Catch what?" I hear Mrs. Webster ask in a worried tone.

"It was heading toward your bedroom, Donnie said," Kayla adds.

"What was?!" Mrs. Webster demands.

"It's probably not venomous, but you never know," Felipe muses.

"WHAT ARE YOU KIDS TALKING ABOUT?" Mrs. Webster demands.

"Oh, well, he promised us free fries if we'd come over and catch the snake that got into your house. We're really good at catching snakes."

Mrs. Webster lets out a shriek that, if we lived in the suburbs, would bring the whole neighborhood running. Luckily out here everything is too far away for anyone to hear.

"Get it! Get it! Kill it!"

Let me stop right here and clear up a few things. One, of course not everyone is terrified of snakes. I just happened to know that Mrs. Webster has a phobia of them. And two, I really hate it when a person's first reaction to a snake is to want to kill it. Snakes are just wild animals trying to get through life without being eaten. Would you want to kill a squirrel or a butterfly? Of course not. Snakes won't chase you. Snakes don't look for people to bite. Most snakes aren't venomous. All of them just want to be left alone. (Except for Boopsnoot, but only because he knows there's a tasty amphibian in his future.)

So I feel a little bad promoting fear of snakes here, but boy, is it ever effective! When I peek through the window I see Mrs. Webster jumping up and down, climbing onto the armchair. She picks up a floor lamp and waves it around like an army of killer snakes has her in their sights.

I really should be proceeding with the next part of our plan, but this is priceless! Boopsnoot (who's pretty nearsighted) is slithering across the living room when he sees the commotion. He immediately does what hognose snakes do—he raises himself up as high as he can, flattens and stretches out his neck so he looks exactly like a cobra, and strikes at the air toward Mrs. Webster.

Hognose snakes are the best actors!

He's just doing it to look big so nothing eats him. But of course Mrs. Webster doesn't know that.

"Wow, it really is a cobra!" Felipe says admiringly. "I didn't believe him."

"Must have escaped from the zoo," Kayla says. "Don't worry, we'll catch him."

As they pretend to round Boopsnoot up, they actually shoo him deeper in the house.

Uh oh, I'd better hurry!

I scurry around the house, peeking into each window. I don't try to hide. I want to be seen. Luckily the Webster house is one story, so I can peer into all of the windows. Finally, in what I guess is a spare bedroom, I see the sickly gray, yellow-spotted alien Speets.

I knock.

I wave.

I grin.

Then I unsling my backpack and pull out Tooba, which I hold gloatingly in front of the window for Speets to see.

CHAPTER 18
POTATO POWER

Speets stares at me for a second, then does a double take. I can almost see the gears in his brain turning and grinding. Ma potpot is in the safe. How did I get it? He looks confused, then furious.

I laugh and point at him mockingly. Then I start to stroll toward the back of the house like I'm going to take the shortcut back to the McKinley property through an empty field. If everything goes according to plan he'll chase me.

Me, and the papier-mâché replica of Tooba we made last night. Turns out making a fake potato is pretty easy. I don't know if you've ever done a papier-mâché project, but pretty much all of them wind up looking like giant potatoes anyway, even if you were really going for a unicorn or a bird.

As I'm leaving, I see Speets get up, all right. But I also see him pick up something that looks suspiciously like a laser gun.

Yikes!

I wanted the other alien to follow me out and chase me for a while, but I never counted on him shooting me with an alien death ray! This just got even more serious!

BLAM—squish!

The alien Speets has tumbled out the back door, and as I turn around he takes a zap at me. Something orange and gooey hits the ground near my feet. I dodge, and another orange splat hits a rosebush.

Oh no! Who knows what that alien goo can do! Luckily, he's only running on his short legs. He doesn't have Plort's bouncing trick. I just need to buy a little more time. Running as fast as I can to the edge of our property, I stop suddenly and face the sneering Speets.

"You want it?" I ask, holding up the replica Tooba. "Well, go and get it, then!" And with all my strength I hurl it into the middle of our potato field. Then I run around him back toward the Webster house.

Just as I hoped, he ignores me and starts trying to climb the fence around the potato fields. But since he has such short legs and arms, I know it's going to take him a while. I just hope it's enough time.

I head to the far side of the house, where Speets can't see me, and peek into the Websters' window again. Kayla and Felipe are in the kitchen, putting on a good show of tackling a dangerous cobra. Boopsnoot is hamming it up, flaring his neck and hissing. I know he's only thinking, *Where's my frog*?

"You wait out there, Mrs. Webster," I hear Felipe say. Then I see Kayla take off her backpack and leave it conveniently next to the big safe.

"Kill it!" Mrs. Webster screams again.

That's when Felipe lunges in and picks up Boopsnoot. "No! It bit me!" he fakes, and just when he lets Boopsnoot go, our gentle snake friend starts the other half of its defensive show.

When a hognose can't bluff its way out of a fight, it plays dead.

Dramatically dead. Hognose snakes are the emotional tweens of the snake kingdom.

Boopsnoot writhes, twisting himself in figure eights. He gapes and shows his belly and twists around like he's in agony. He even sprays snake musk, which the Websters are going to remember for a *really* long time. Then, with one last hiss, he lets his tongue loll out, foams at the mouth, and lies still.

"There," Kayla says, gently picking up the limp Boopsnoot. "Saved the day."

Mrs. Webster is too upset. "I'm going to my room to lie down," she says, and staggers off.

"We'll just take him out the back," Felipe says as, with perfect timing, Donnie and a tiny figure in a bright yellow raincoat come up the front walkway.

I listen as Donnie talks.

"My dad said no one is supposed to open the safe, ever. What do you need to see it for, anyway?"

"Bad neighbor Spud make trouble."

"Yeah, he's a trouble-making jerk," Donnie agrees. What, *me*? "How come you're talking all funny?"

Plort pushes back his hood, showing his painted gray-and-yellow skin, and points to the translator on his head. "Fell in waterfall, broke."

"Waterfall? Oh, you took a shower. Whatever. Look Speets, I'm not very happy about what's going on. You made the deal with me. All the candy I can eat—a lifetime supply. You said space candy is like nothing I've ever tasted before. Then when my dad saw you, you made a new deal with him. That's not fair. Forget what you promised him. I want my candy or you're not ever getting this stupid alien potato."

He traded an entire species' safety for candy? Doesn't surprise me.

"Okay, Plor . . . er, Speets trade. You give potpot, I get candy."

But Donnie isn't stupid. Well, not completely. "No way. Candy first, then the potato."

"Okay, but you show potpot. Check potpot, then get candy."

Donnie seems okay with this. He hasn't checked on his mom, and he doesn't hear Kayla and Felipe (and Boopsnoot) sneaking to the back of the house to let me in. I'm peeking around the corner when the safe door swings open. "There, satisfied?" Donnie asks, and he's just about to slam it closed when I jump out.

"Give me back my potato, you thief!" I shout. Then I ball up my fists like I'm going to fight him. (I've never thrown a punch in my life.)

Donnie snarls at me and immediately runs at me.

Plort, disguised as Speets, is left in front of the open safe.

It doesn't take a lot of acting for me to look terrified when Donnie charges toward me. He's a big guy, as tall as I am and about twice as thick. He looks like he's been brawling since preschool. With a frightened gasp I whirl around and run. Kayla and Felipe have ducked into the hall bathroom, and Donnie chases me right past them without noticing. As soon as I lead Donnie away they can sneak back to the kitchen and take Tooba out of the safe.

All part of the plan.

It's *not* part of the plan when I run smack into Speets, who just came back inside. I do a complete flip and go sprawling, with Speets wiggling and screeching underneath me. He's cold, squishy, and slippery, like a giant curd of cottage cheese. Tucked under the other arm is the papier-mâché Tooba. "Fake!" Speets screeches, and hurls the make-believe Tooba against the wall, where it cracks, showing its hollow insides. Then he tries to stand up, obviously intending to charge at Plort.

I make a grab for the alien but just manage to catch

his legs, tripping him. His translator flies off his head and skitters toward the kitchen.

"SPEETS spats sports!" the alien shouts furiously. "Sprats! Speets-speets!"

Donnie skids to a halt. "Wait a minute," he says, a little slow on the uptake. "If you're Speets, then who's . . ." We all look behind him to the kitchen, where Plort—his paint starting to peel—stands proudly holding Ma Potpot.

"Speets!" the bad alien screeches, and kicks free of me.

"What the . . . ?" Donnie says. "Get out of my house!" He starts toward me, then decides it might be in his best interests to help Speets protect the alien potato. But as he runs to help him, Kayla sticks a foot out of the bathroom and trips him. While Felipe holds Boopsnoot safely out of danger, I leap over Donnie and run into the kitchen.

Suddenly there are four kids and two aliens in a small kitchen playing a very serious game of Hot Potato!

Speets slaps it out of Plort's hand. As it rolls along the ground I grab it, but then Donnie shoves me and I throw it to Felipe . . . forgetting his hands are full of snake. It hits his chest and rolls to the ground, where Kayla and Donnie scramble for it.

"Got it!" Donnie shouts, before Speets grabs it out of his hands. "Hey, you're on my side!"

Before anyone can get to him, Speets throws the potato into the microwave and turns it on the highest power. "Speets, speets splurts! *Splat!*" He laughs wickedly and pulls the goo gun from a holster at his hip. We all cringe back as poor Tooba rotates in the microwave.

"What did he say, Plort?" I ask.

"Badspeets say, if he can't have ma potpot, no one have ma potpot." Plort looks at me in despair. "Say without ma potpot, everyplort doomed!"

Just then, my beloved Tooba, Plort's own precious ma potpot, explodes in the microwave.

"Now get out!" Donnie shouts at us.

He doesn't have to tell us twice! We run past him through the kitchen toward the front door. As Kayla passes she ducks down to retrieve the backpack she left by the safe.

Then, fast as we can, we run back to my house.

"Thanks, Boopsnoot," I say as I let him go in the leaf littler behind the firewood.

“Well, that didn’t go exactly as planned,” I say when I get back to my room, where Felipe, Kayla, and Plort are waiting for me.

“Not exactly,” Plort says in flawless, high-pitched English. “In fact, it went even better!”

He points to the translator on his head—in perfect condition. “I swiped Speets’s translator,” Plort says.

“That’s fantastic, Plort!” I say, beaming. “A shame about ma potpot, though.”

Apparently Donnie isn’t smart enough to realize that a potato doesn’t explode in a microwave in under a minute.

However, a papier-mâché potato does.

I told you they were easy to make. So easy, in fact, that we made three of them.

One for Speets.

One hidden in Kayla’s bag, planted next to the safe for Plort to switch. The real ma potpot ended up in Kayla’s bag as we ran out of the house.

And one fake potpot that now rests happily in the hydroponic chamber in the barn to trick my parents—and any would-be thieves—for a while.

Later that day, Kayla and Felipe pedal home with the real ma potpot. It will be safe, for now, in her laboratory. "Just don't let the centipedes and earwigs get it!" I warn her as they leave.

It was an exciting, scary day, but I'm happy. We really pulled it off. And I couldn't have done it without my three best friends.

My parents are happy, too. Today was even better than Saturday. They made a ton of money. For now, they have plenty of slime, and all the potatoes that are still growing.

Maybe that will be enough to make up for not having Tooba. I've decided once and for all that I'm giving Tooba to Plort.

Because now that he has the working translator, he can tell me the whole story.

CHAPTER 19

IF AT FIRST YOU DON'T SUCCEED, FRY, FRY AGAIN!

One good thing about aliens, goo-guns, and evil space generals—they put things in perspective. After yesterday, middle school doesn't seem like such a terrible thing. I don't think it's going to be much fun, but I think I can handle it.

Now, when I wake up bright and early Monday morning, I have much worse things on my mind than middle school. Middle school will be a walk in the park by comparison. Sure, more like a sweltering, mosquito-infested park filled with angry geese than a pretty garden. But still, nothing I can't handle.

As for the rest of my life, I'm not so sure.

Last night, with Speets's translator, Plort was able

to tell us the complete story of how and why he came to Earth.

Plort's people live on a pleasant, peaceful planet that orbits a yellow dwarf star much like our own sun. It is a land of green rivers and blue trees, where the warblebeasts sing their magical songs as they migrate across vast savannas of silver sedge. The Plorts lived happy, bouncy lives.

Until General Tantrunium and his minions came. The general was looking for a vacation home, and Planet Plort suited him perfectly. Unfortunately it was infested with vermin—that's what he called Plort's people. He thought it would be an easy matter to destroy them. But he didn't know about the pot-pots.

Before the general came, Plort's people had no real concept of war. But they did love sports! They discovered centuries ago that if they mixed their pot-pots with a semisentient slime that is abundant on their planet, it would make the plorts grow huge and strong. What's more, it would give them a force field that would protect them from any attack.

Another species might have used this as a weapon and conquered other planets.

Instead, the Plorts built a huge stadium and played passionate games of Bounceball. It is their favorite Plort sport. After eating the slime-coated potpots, Plort athletes would play a game something like football, something like rugby, but about twenty times more violent. Only no one got hurt, of course, because they were protected by the saucy potpots.

When General Tantrunium came to their planet with his bulldozers and architects to build his vacation home, the Plorts welcomed him. Unfortunately, the Plort words for welcome translated into Tantrunium's language as "Get lost, you ugly creep!"

So in a fit of rage, Tantrunium destroyed their capital city.

The shocked Plorts fought back the only way they could—every citizen ate the potpots and slime, and grew to humongous proportions. General Tantrunium was defeated!

But he was determined, and kept launching attacks. Over and over, the Plorts beat Tantrunium's army. But the potpot supplies were running dangerously low. They'd only been used for Bounceball before. After a year of fighting, there were almost none left.

Our friend, a private in the hastily assembled citizen's army, was one of many Plorts charged with secretly bringing the precious ma potpots to other planets to see if they could reproduce there. Only some of the potpots could make new ones—just the special ma potpots.

But General Tantrunium, hearing about this through one of his spies, caught all of the Plorts carrying potpots. All but one. Then he poisoned every remaining potpot on Planet Plort.

Our friend Plort got an urgent message to rush his potpot back to his home planet. It was the last one—the only chance to save his people! But he panicked and took a dangerous detour through our solar system. His ship hit the sun's gravitational field and was flung into the asteroid belt. He escaped in a pod, but his ma potpot was jettisoned. Last he saw it, it was careening toward Earth.

"I was banished from my planet," Plort told us, hanging his head. "Through my reckless behavior, I let my people down. But I thought I could redeem myself. I stole a ship and headed straight back to Earth to find ma potpot. If I could get her home, we could breed new ma potpots. But now I've failed again."

He told us that now General Tantrunium is going to destroy his people. “They’ll be rounded up, sent to a prison planet to work in the mines! He’s only waiting to make sure all of the potpots on Planet Plort are really dead. As soon as he knows there will be no resistance, he’ll attack!”

And there won’t be any resistance . . . unless we can get ma potpot back to his planet. Then his people’s scientists can grow new ma potpots to replace the ones Tantrunium poisoned.

“But there’s no way I can do that now!” Plort told us as he paced back and forth in my bedroom. “My ship was damaged in the crash. I can’t get home.”

“Maybe I can do something about that,” Kayla told him.

Plort looked hopeful for a split second. Then his face fell. “It won’t do any good. You can’t fix it fast enough. I threw General Tantrunium off my track with a gamma particle dissipater. But it is only a matter of time before he can trace my path. I thought I could land on Earth, find ma potpot, and get home before he found me. I’m such a failure!”

“No, you’re not, Plort,” I told him. “Don’t worry. We’ll figure something out.”

“Will we recognize this General Tantrunium when we see him?” Felipe asked.

Plort nodded. “He’s disgusting. He’s gross. He’s mean.”

“So far you could be describing Donnie Webster,” I quipped.

Plort glares at me. “You won’t laugh when he’s here, Spud. When you see the general’s purple slime, you know you’re *doomed*!”

Like I’m going to get any sleep after news like that!

• • •

Now it’s morning, first day of school. Felipe and Kayla went home—their parents drew the line at three sleepovers in a row—so now just Plort and I are getting ready for the first day of sixth grade. I don’t have time to be nervous for this milestone anymore, not when I have to figure out how to take care of my new alien friend and worry about a pending evil alien invasion.

“I can’t leave you home,” I tell him. “What if my parents find you?”

“I’d rather your parents find me than General Tantrunium," Plort says, trembling. "You don't understand what he'll do to me! To anyone who helps me. He's merciless!"

Yup, this makes middle school look like a piece of cake.

Mom and Dad have excused me from potato duties this morning, just for the first day. So at 7:15 (I couldn't sleep so I might as well get there early) I let Plort hop in my backpack and head to school.

As I pedal up, I can't help but think that Solanum Middle School looks *huge*! I went there on a field trip in fifth grade, but I forgot how big it is. Three different elementary schools feed into it—Solanum Primary, and schools from the neighboring towns of Erdapfel and Murphy.

Even the lawn in front of the school is crowded, chaotic, and loud. I can feel Plort shifting uneasily in my backpack. I start to wonder if bringing him was the best idea. What will my new classmates think when they see a kid who smells like potatoes carrying a bag that wiggles?

But, oh, there are Kayla and Felipe, riding up on their bikes. They live just a few minutes away from school. As we lock our bikes, Felipe leans over and whispers,

"What are we going to do if the general shows up?"

I look at the masses of kids flowing into the school, most of them so much bigger than me, with zits and facial hair, and take a deep breath. "I'm not even going to think about that now. Let's just get through today. Do you remember where anything is?"

"All I remember is where the cafeteria is!" Felipe laughs.

"And I just remember the library!" Kayla says.

It feels so good to have my best friends with me. As we walk in together I feel almost happy, almost confident, almost comfortable. . . .

Until something hits my cheek with a solid, wet *splat*. I turn around, thinking for a second that I'm under attack from General Tantrunium.

Nope. Just Donnie Webster with a straw and a huge evil grin. He's wearing an oversized backpack—and it wiggles. I hear a squeak from inside, kind of like Plort's but mocking and malicious. I wipe my face and find a disgusting spitball. With a grimace of distaste I shake it onto the floor.

"No littering!" barks a woman with a name tag labeling her as the assistant principal. "Next time you do that you're getting written up!"

"But I . . ."

Just then the first bell rings. We only have a few minutes to get to class. The assistant principal stalks away. Across the hall, Donnie points and laughs, joking with some new friends who look like they belong in high school. One even has a wispy mustache!

"Don't even think about that bully," Kayla says. "As long as we stick together . . ."

Behind us, Felipe gasps and drops his bag.

He's looking at the big soccer field on the side of the school.

"Oh no!" Kayla whispers, grabbing my arm.

"What is it?" Plort asks from inside my bag. I don't even care if anyone can hear him.

Barely able to breathe, I say, "There's purple slime all over the soccer field! General Tantrunium is here!"

"Ma potpot preserve us!" Plort squeaks. Then there's a little thud inside my backpack. I'm pretty sure Plort has passed out.

I stare at the slime-covered field, feeling my lower lip quiver. But I take a deep breath and press my lips together. I'm going to be strong. I'm going to save Plort.

But who's going to save me?

All I know is there's only one potato that can save us now. With Tooba's help, maybe my friends and I can show this nasty General Tantrunium who's the real Lord of the Fries!

But first, middle school.

TO BE CONTINUED

L. S. KINNEDY grew up in Upstate New York and spent long nights waiting for aliens to visit. But aliens are always late, so Kinnedy used that time to start writing stories. Today, Kinnedy loves bike riding, catching snakes, poking around creeks . . . you know, the fun stuff most people forget about after middle school. Kinnedy's favorite potato food is *pommes frites*, which is how snooty grown-ups say French fries.